I've
Seen
Dry

by

Kent Elliott

This is a work of fiction. Characters, incidents, settings and dialogue are drawn from the author's imagination. With the exception of certain public figures and organizations of the time, any resemblance to actual events or persons, living or dead, is not to be construed as real. If a reader makes a connection between a character or event and some real person or event, that reader will undoubtedly add "but he got it/her/him wrong." It's fiction.

Wheatgrass Publishing (a personal imprint), Boulder, Montana

ISBN: 0615799124

ISBN-13: 978-0615799124

For Barb

ACKNOWLEDGMENTS

Thanks:

First of all to Barb for her support and tolerance as I went off to live among my made up characters every day.

To family members who read and encouraged along the way: Sarah, Heather, Hannah, Susan, and Lynn.

To Jan Townsend for providing pictures that helped me recall the texture and grandeur of the open prairie land; and get a feeling for the challenges faced by early settlers.

To Bill Selby, for observations on the relationship systems developed in the story, including discomfort that conversations became public so quickly.

To the North Jefferson County Writers' Group.

To the host of friends who kept asking, "How's the book coming." And for adding their desire to read it.

1

"I'm the oldest, you know."

Madge had been a member of the Harstad Community Church ever since she came to town to marry Mr. Carter and help him run the Mercantile in the 1920's. On this warm August Sunday Madge sat through the worship service with her eyes closed—except during the hymns. She didn't try to sing, but filled the time while others sang with the slow, arduous activity of standing up and fumbling with the hymn book. As an amen was sung she reversed the process, slowing seating herself in the third pew from the front. From my place in the pulpit I looked at Madge and thought I saw a sleeping elder while I preached the sermon. I would soon learn something about that assumption.

"I'm the oldest, you know."

Madge's refrain rang into the church's suddenly quiet sanctuary. The worship center had been filled with the music of an organ postlude. The final chord sounded just as she finally reached the big double doors at the back of the sunlit worship room with its large frosted glass windows, its bleached oak furniture and white walls. I stood in that open doorway

1

shaking hands with the departing church-goers as they welcomed me, the newly arrived pastor in their community. Down the aisle of the bright worship center, toward the dim front hallway cloak room (in churchy words we'd say 'from sanctuary to narthex') on the way to social hall coffee time, Madge inched her way slowly toward me. Her walker clicked noisily as she made her way. Her elbows jutted out sideways, making her physical presence wider than seemed possible. She had shrunk with the long years, yet she somehow filled the center aisle. Tiny as she was, under five feet tall, between elbows and walker, no child could slip past her to get to the cookies before she had completed her journey from pew to narthex and greeted me with a hand shake.

So she said it again, "I'm the oldest, you know."

As Ed and Karl got ready to help Madge negotiate the steps, Nilda caught up with us. Nilda and Madge both lived at Prairie Manor, the local nursing home. Nilda whispered as she shook my hand, "Madge'll tell you that all the time. I guess it's just because she's survived a lot." And she, too, left me to greet others, and to wonder.

***

While Madge was helped to the sidewalk and a ride to dinnertime at the Manor, most of us headed down the long staircase to the church basement. For many, this time of socializing over coffee and cookies was more the main event than the church service. On this day I may have had a full cup of coffee with each conversation cluster as I mingled and listened, intent on getting well acquainted with as many as possible.

I was the last to leave the building. My family—Roberta and our two little daughters—had left earlier in the car. I would make my way the six blocks home on foot. I thought everyone had gone but I found Karl waiting outside in a small area of precious mid-day shade at the northeast corner of the building. When he noticed me, he stepped from this shelter onto the sidewalk to face the redwood plank sign mounted parallel to the street. He pointed to the area at the bottom, where a plank had been removed. With a gesture, Karl beckoned me to join him. "I told Sherm I'd help him do the new plank with your name, Pastor Wil. You've met Mr. Sherman, haven't you?" I nodded as Karl continued, "He's good with a router, but I don't trust him to follow the lettering stencils. He might try to be too creative, so I want to be there when we cut it. What should the plank say? Just your name, or what?"

"What did the last one say?" I asked.

"Well, let's see. I've walked past that sign so often I don't really see it anymore, I guess. I think it had Pastor Tim's name, middle initial maybe, and, now I remember that it said 'Minister' not 'Pastor' even though he always like to be called Pastor Tim. And it had the parsonage phone number, too."

"Did he ever regret having the home phone number on there?"

"Oh, I don't think so. It's in the book, anyway."

"Well, let's stick with tradition, then. Have it say, 'Wilford G. Wilson, Minister' and the phone. Even though you all are already calling me Pastor Wil."

"Sounds good. Maybe 'Wilford G. (Pastor Wil) Wilson'?" He cupped his hands in front of him to indicate the parentheses.

"I don't think so. By the way, were you waiting for me in the heat of the day, just to talk about the sign?"

"No. Not really. I'm waiting for Frieda. She took Madge home to the Manor. And she should have been back here and then some by now." Just then we heard the car, and watched as Frieda turned the corner. "And speak of the devil's wife, here she comes."

"Did Frieda take Nilda, too?"

"No. Just Madge. Ed usually drives her, but he had to go right to some family doings today. I don't know who carries Nilda back and forth."

Frieda pulled the Pontiac up to the curb beside us. Karl was ready to jump in on the passenger side, but by then Frieda was out of the car and trotting toward us in shoes of a design to discourage attempts to move fast.

As she was catching her breath, Frieda said, "Oh! Pastor, I have to tell you. Madge was so full of stories today, I just couldn't leave. I sat with her all through her dinner; which she hardly ate, she was talking so much. Anyway, she first asked me what your sermon was about. I kidded with her about sleeping through church again. She told me how no one believes her when she says that isn't true. Then she told me all about it. Sitting in church she went on a trip through time. She told me about her homestead just across the Dakota line. She told how her family's farm had survived the price fixing by railroads and Minnesota milling tycoons; and how, for enough years it had survived through wet and dry. She said the farm had even outlasted the killing. But she wouldn't say anything more about what that was. She talked about "big biz" power that kept them poor. And how weather and low wheat prices caused the debt that finally left it broke. Madge was in kind of a reverie while she told me about her daydreams in church. Those dreams took her back to younger days. She said she wasn't really sure anymore whether she came into town to marry and then took to keeping store, or if she came for the work and just settled in with Mr. Carter. We had such a good time with her talking on and me yes-nodding, thinking about how tough she is, still living with such joy after all that hardship."

"Wow!" I said. "Thank you for telling us about that, Frieda. Amazing! If what I heard someone at the seminary say is true, that the art of sermon listening is creative mind wandering, then Madge gets an 'A' today. She's the oldest, you know."

"Have a good week, Pastor," Frieda said with grin. "See you later."

Karl waved and headed around to the driver's door, opened it and stopped, then called over the top of the car, "Need a lift home, Wil?"

It was a hot day, and since my family had long since taken our junker Renault 12 home. I accepted the ride. We rode the few blocks in silence. I couldn't bring myself to ask Karl about his startled expression when Frieda had told us Madge's farm had even survived the killing.

***

By the time I got home Berta and the kids had finished their lunch. Ruthie had gone down the street to a new friend's house and Rebecca was taking her nap. I found the last of the soup on the stove, ready to re-heat. When Berta joined me at the table I pre-empted her critique of my sermon by reporting what Frieda had said about Madge's time travels. "She said Madge mentioned a killing, but that's all she would say about it. I wonder about that. I've got to find out about that history."

Berta, who knows me too well, said, "Why do you think you have to know about a killing? Is that your job? You're not a cop, and it was probably a farm accident. Besides, I got a chance to meet old Madge—she's the oldest, you know. She told me that twice in the five minutes we talked. But in between I saw a woman who lives reasonably well in the present—at least when her eyes are open. And they seem open to the real world around us. She had nice things to say about Ruthie and Rebecca, too. Not trite things, either. Of course, with her ninety year old ears she probably didn't hear all the uproar they were making a few rows behind her."

If I was supposed to ask "what were the nice things she said," I missed the cue. Instead I defended my desire to know about a killing. "Yeah, you know I love mystery stories. But that's not all of it. She might just need to talk about those times to someone who hasn't already heard it. And it sounds like there was a pivotal event that may need to come out. There is pastoral care in what I intend, you see."

"Well, go for it. But be careful," she said. "Madge is a precious elderly lady, so take care of her. Your soup is getting cold. Better go ahead and eat it." With that, shaking her head at the way I rationalize motives, she left the kitchen. I was left to lunch with my thoughts.

2

When our little singing group arrived at the Manor for the weekly "Songs before Supper" that Tuesday, I looked for the two residents I had met. Madge was seated in an overstuffed vinyl chair in a sunlit corner of the large room. Nilda, a substantial woman, tall and just plain big, sat at a table in the dining end of the large room. Nilda had made a comment about Madge on the way out of church, but the women didn't seem to acknowledge each other. It had me thinking that maybe there really is a pastoral care need, and maybe it's with Nilda.

"Smiles" was just another of the many songs-from-before-my-time that I would learn as we sang. But then I saw the tears. Something in the lyric or a memory was affecting Madge in a way that had me intrigued and anxious to learn, if I could, more of her story. What had she survived to become the proud oldest? I resolved in that moment, as we sang those old Tin Pan Alley songs, that I would be back before the week was out for a visit.

There are smiles that make us happy,
There are smiles that make us blue,
There are smiles that steal away the teardrops,

As the sunbeams steal away the dew.
There are smiles that have a tender meaning,
That the eyes of love alone may see,
And the smiles that fill my life with sunshine
Are the smiles that you give to me. *

***

Rachel, who led our group, caught up to me on the way to the parking area after the singing. She pulled me aside and said, "I think Madge and Nilda are about the only residents here who get out to our church, but I don't think they're friends. You never see them together. That always bothers me somehow. Maybe you could..."

I interrupted, "I did notice that. And I saw something that convinced me that I'll come back to visit with Madge very soon. And it looks like I'll visit Nilda, too."

"Oh, good. I guess that's what I was hoping to get you to do. I want to ask what that 'something' is, but I do know better." With that she waved a good-bye and dashed for her car.

---

* Music: Lee S. Roberts; Words: J. Will Callahan. 1917

3

I found Madge in her favorite comfy chair (if Naugahyde can ever be comfy) in a sunny corner of Prairie Manor's only sitting room. It was a large room. One end was used for dining, and at the other was a comfortable seating area. A long south wall was practically all window, looking out across a paved patio toward a long retaining wall against the hillside. Grade school children, attempting to brighten the view for their elderly friends, had covered the concrete wall with many painted pictures. I supposed I should be grateful for this kindly gift, even though, to my eyes the result was god-awful graffiti.

After greeting Madge, re-introducing myself as I would continue to do, I trotted across the room and grabbed a chair from a table. I pushed her walker aside in order to sit facing her directly and, I hoped, be heard. I had no idea how to get our conversation there, but I longed to learn how it was that "Smiles" brought tears. Where to begin, though?

We can always start with the weather. Even if she's unaware of outside conditions in her diminished time of life, I suspected her farming experience could make it a worthy topic. So I opened, "This drought is getting real bad this summer. Have you ever seen it so dry?"

Her silent response of several gentle nods of the head seemed deeper than simply not hearing. I waited, but then went on, a little louder: "I'm told the wheat should be heavy and heading out by now. We were driving along the Jabbok Road the other day. And I'm not exaggerating. The wheat is short and the stalks are so sparse, there's just one little blade where a seed was planted. You could sight & shoot a 30-06 between the stems and never hit a stalk of wheat. Have you ever seen it so dry?"

Finally Madge looked me in the eye and spoke, "I've seen dry and I've seen wet. It was dry that brought us to town. By 1921 we were getting some better rain, but it was too late. Rain was spotty out there. Some had a decent crop, but not us. With hardly a crop and mortgaged to the limit we didn't even have enough to seed in '21.

"It was me and the youngsters then. My oldest, his name is Bertram but we call him Buddy, anyway he was fifteen at the time, becoming a real man. And he had to grow up early. They all did, after the killing. There was Buddy and Ralph, just a year younger. Then the girls, Pearl and Cynthia. And Peter was still just a baby when Elwin died.

"Buddy and Ralph tried so hard to keep that farm going. Ready to fight for it just like their Pop. I guess it was mostly for their Pop's honor that they had that hunger to keep the farm. Sometimes we were really ragged. A dry year, when even the little house garden didn't produce, we'd be hurting, but those boys still had a hunger for the farm that was deeper. That their daddy didn't die in vain, I suppose you'd call it. But the League was getting weaker by then and not much help. It couldn't inspire them in any way that could make a difference. That was in '21, I believe."

As her story began to unfold, there were so many questions I needed to ask. Elwin's death? The League? But not yet. Madge was still telling it her way.

"Yes, '21 it was. We were just dug in too deep. A little nice spring rain but nothing to plant. It was just too much by then. So the bank finally got us. And those boys of mine were ready to take the bankers to war, I tell you. Thank God for Mr. Carter." And Madge breathed a long, slow, sighing breath.

After a quiet moment, she continued, brightening a bit. "Mr. Carter. He had a way with words. He could convince a coyote to eat sagebrush instead of the lamb right in front of it. He settled those boys. Even convinced Ralph and Pearl to go to high school. Oh, and wasn't that a blessing. Cynthia and Peter, coming up behind, stayed in school with never a question about it. So we left the farm, came to town and Mr. Carter's Mercantile."

Madge closed her eyes then, and seemed to doze off. It seemed to be time to leave and let her rest. I started to get up. My chair scraped along the tile floor as I pushed back, startling Madge back into wakefulness. She didn't seem to notice that I was getting up to leave. I sat back down as she resumed her reminiscences in a kind of reverie.

***

"That was the prettiest farm you ever did see. You'll have to take a drive out there one day, Pastor. The creek, when it's running water in springtime.." Before she continued, Madge closed her eyes for a moment with that unfinished thought.

"In springtime, oh yes, then it's a real stream of water. The big old cottonwoods; the hills and wide range; the wind through the grass and sage. You see the storms build in the northwest and then come crashing over you from the south. Even when it was so cold your breath froze on your lips, when the snowdrifts piled high. Even then, after the blizzard and the sun was blinding on a sea of pure white, even then that was the prettiest place. You take a drive out there, you'll see."

I asked then, "Would you like to go along and show it to me?"

Her answer let me know I wasn't supposed to interrupt, and also something of the depth of her struggle in telling me so much. A tear came to her right eye as she said, "No. It isn't a place I can look at again. We buried Elwin on the hill there. Would you see if the marker is still there, just a ways up the slope on top of a sandstone rim a couple hundred yards from the dam? Look for the marker, would you?

"You go out the Sage City Road. About thirty miles after you leave the pavement. You cross the Dakota line soon after, but there's no sign, just a cattle guard and fence row. You'll see miles of flat, lovely wheat land, and some cut bank and a little badland country that's no good for crops, though we tried. There's good grass to grow the calves into fine beef steers in that rougher country, though. Anyway, you go out there, you'll come up a long hill and as you crest that hill you'll right away know that I'm telling it true. That's the prettiest farmstead on the prairie. Right after you crest that hill, there'll be a track leading off to your right down into the cottonwoods where we staked our homestead claim. The little frame house is long gone. But you can still find where we started, where we built the sod house in the cut bank there. You're too young to know a thing about living in a soddy. You got any idea what to look for? Don't be too blind to find it. It's still there if you look. Built right into the side of the cut bank, as close to the creek as we dared. Gilead Creek isn't much out there, more a likely place to drill a well than a stream of water, especially at this time of year. It is August now, ain't it?"

I nodded, "Yes, today is August 14, 1981. I will try to find your place out Gilead Creek." At the time, I had no idea there was a Gilead Creek. I hadn't even heard of Sage County, so finding them was not at all certain in my mind. Repeated instructions before we parted still didn't give me any greater confidence about finding it.

Before we said goodbye, Madge added, "I told you, didn't I, come over the top of that long hill, and there'll be a wagon track on your right. But I believe the grandkids said the barbed wire fence doesn't even have a gate in there anymore. So, you'll have to climb through there, and just walk down that track. First you'll come to a little dam we built there. I'm sure they still keep that up, for the stock to drink from. If there's cattle drinking from that dam, just stay out of their way. Then follow along the creek and keep an eye on the cut bank for the homestead dugout. It's the prettiest place! Truth be told, though, it's maybe prettied up in my memories. 'cause I'm the oldest you know." She said that last with a twinkle in her eye that also conveyed that her signature line meant it was time for me to get along home.

4

I'd been unable to be with our Tuesday singing group so it was a week later that I next visited the Manor. This time I found Madge sitting in a small armchair in her room. The second bed in the room was stripped to a bare mattress and there were no personal belongings at that side of the room. Even so, nothing was said about her roommate's departure, nothing about a roommate at all.

At Madge's side of the room, one large color photograph dominated an otherwise blank blue wall. There were other snapshots crowded together, propped and piled on a chest of drawers, but the large photo held my attention. It showed a large group, at least a hundred people, with family unit clusters crowded into a group portrait on a grassy hillside. Madge, at the very front and center, sat in a folding picnic arm chair. Clearly, this was the official portrait of a family reunion at which Madge was matriarch. I intended to inquire, that she might tell about the event and family gatherings. My eyes kept being drawn to the picture while she told the story as she intended to tell it. Again and again, Madge would make it clear that leading questions were unnecessary distractions.

The day was chilly and brought with it nearly an inch of rain that broke a summer long dry spell, so Madge seemed ready to begin our conversation with the weather.

Pulling off my damp green and yellow John Deere tractor cap as I sat down, I shook it, spraying both of us. I set it on my knee, apologizing, "Sorry. I'm like a dog coming out of a swimming hole I guess. Got to share the moisture with everybody. They say this rain is what little is left of the hurricane that hit Texas."

Madge seemed more grateful than annoyed about the accidental spray and ready for some storytelling. "I've seen dry, but I've seen wet, too. All those years working with Mr. Carter at the Mercantile and I guess I'm still a farmer at heart. Years when it does rain, those are the good years out here. I always wonder what Elwin might think of us, of what became of us. Storekeepers. Did we betray him, do you think?"

I couldn't possibly answer that. So I didn't try. I just shrugged and let Madge continue.

"It's my farmer way, you see. I remember the store years, the indoor work as wet years. Life is better with a little money so you know there'll be enough to feed all the family next week, too. I still miss the farm, but Mr. Carter did right by us."

I had to ask, "You refer to your husband—God rest his soul—as Mr. Carter. Didn't you tell me you had three more children with him? I can't help but wonder about that. What was his first name?"

Madge replied, "Charles. Oh well, I suppose it might seem odd. Mr. Carter did right by us. He put Buddy to work making deliveries to the ranches and farms all around. That kept Buddy close to what he loved. Driving and fixing, lots of fixing. That Model T truck wasn't so different, so Buddy claimed, not so different from running the Ford tractor that he bought with that last loan the bank would ever give us—the tractor they took back.

"And Ralph, always with his nose in a book, got to go to school every day. After the killing there was always so much work for those two oldest, my strong boys, out on the farm. It was hard to get them to school. The little ones was good about going to our country school. And in time they got accustomed to the big town school with four classrooms instead of one for the eight grades. We never even considered schooling after grammar school graduation until Mr. Carter helped get Ralph and Pearl into the high school. Ralph thought he was in heaven, let me tell you. He's our scholar, caught up in no time though he'd missed too much to have an elementary diploma to bring with him. Mr. Carter was on the school board at the time, so he had strings he could pull, and he did.

"Those turn out to be the wet years. Oh, the weather was just as unpredictable as ever, but we had a more steady, settled way of life. Looking back it all seems so steady and settled. I didn't think so at the time, when the Depression hit. But we worked hard every day. Between the store, my ragamuffins and the babies. Did I tell you about my second family? Mr. Carter might have been old – he was fifteen years older that Elwin would've been, but he loved me and I appreciated him, too.

"Maralta was the prettiest baby you ever did see, almost prettier than Cynthia. Cynthy was nine or ten that year. But Maralta hardly had a chance. She was barely one when the fever took her. Oh, I hurt more losing her than I did losing Elwin, I sometimes feel. I miss Elwin. But I still have dreams about Maralta—who she might've become.

"Henry and Ruth were pretty babies, too. And I loved them. But did I do right by them, still grieving as I was? Every chance I had, between the Mercantile, cooking and washing and all the chores a woman had in those days....every chance, I would be at that Free sewing machine that Mr. Carter bought for us. Free was a make of sewing machine. Mr. Carter did have to pay money for it. I loved to sew for my girls, and made better than store bought for my boys, too."

I interrupted, saying, "I know. My grandmother had a Free-Westinghouse."

"Well, later I had one of them, too, with the electric motor and no more dancing on the treadle. I'm telling you about the good years, don't you know. Because you seem to be paying attention. I know you'll come back so I can tell about the hard times, too."

I took this as a signal that Madge must be tired and I could leave her to visit Nilda before I left the Manor. But apparently not yet.

As I began to stand up, Madge signaled me back down. "Sit down Pastor. I said I'm telling you about the good years.

"The Depression was hard, hard on everybody. More farms and ranches lost, but others—the smarter farmers or the lucky ones—bought up the land cheap and put together holdings that carried them through. I would never tell this to Mr. Carter. It was always his store and he was the business boss, but I think it was my gift for sewing that saw us through those years. He always had yard goods for sale, but I made it into something, a real department of the Merc. Those years when money was so scarce, I taught the women how to dress their families nice from the cheap, but stylish cloth we sold. Maybe I take too much credit. My girls wearing those nice homemade clothes brought in the customers. Early on, we started a pattern exchange. Folks would bring their used patterns back to the store. We'd mark what size they cut it. In the thirties we made that a free service, as long as they came to us for their yard goods and notions. I truly believe that's what kept our doors open when others couldn't. Oh, Mr. Carter would say it was selling the big items like a new sewing machine or an Aermotor windmill now and then that kept us going. Let him. He had to string out the payments on those sales, without much interest, for so long that you couldn't see any profit by the end. Yes, we did alright. And we all took care of each other in those days. We were a long way away from the troubles in the big cities. Still, the railroads had us in their back pocket and that was still just as sore for us as it was before the killing."

My mouth opened, about to ask a direct question about the killing, about what that meant, but Madge patted me on the knee that didn't have my cap resting and drying on it. Somehow, she managed to stop the question before it came out.

"I hope you'll come back. Maybe I'll tell you some about Elwin. By the way, have you been out to look at our place out Gilead Creek?"

"Not yet," was the best I could offer. I was still trying to find the area on a map. I needed county maps in two states....and besides, I was putting it off.

Madge sent me away with the advice, "Don't go out today. You'll sink in the gumbo mud and never be seen again."

***

Looking at the time, I determined to slip away without visiting Nilda. It was a good plan, but of course it didn't work. Nilda was just coming out of the large room with the big south windows, heading toward her single room. There was no avoiding her now. Our previous visits in the short time since I came to town had been at church or by telephone. I knew that I should give her some attention, but it was already uncomfortable for me because she always seemed so needy. I had to remind myself that this was part of the job I'd signed on to do.

Nilda led me to her room. There were things she wanted to show me; and I was amazed. The walls were covered with photographs, typewritten letters, ribbons – a massive clutter of memorabilia. There were just a few family photos—black and white portraits of stern, unsmiling family, and more recent color snapshots with children at play. On prominent display were 8x10 signed glossies of some of Montana's best known politicians. Check that—of Democratic politicians. In a region dominated by Republicans, I had found a proud, partisan Democrat.

For the second time that day, expecting that family photos would open a conversation, something else intruded. Instead, pointing to the picture signed by Lee Metcalf, I recalled to her a time I stood in a buffet line chatting with the Senator and his wife, then added, "You really have some strong political

17

connections. What makes you a Democrat in eastern Montana?"

Nilda grunted and said, "I wasn't always a Democrat, or anything else for that matter. Always will be now, though, I guess. There was a time in Kirchen County when you could stand up and say you're a proud Democrat and people wouldn't laugh. Now it's all Republicans in charge, and they don't even know their own history. That's just the way it was. Maybe we Democrats are a better party now than we were back then. I say we, but I wasn't much interested in politics until later years. Like it is with so many others, FDR gets the credit. It would be even better with more Democrats, but maybe Harstad is a better town now. The railroad put in the dams and watering ponds that started the town. The rail company figured they owned the town. Lots of farmers would say the railroad owned them, too. My Papa was real political, opinionated that is, and it stung him. He always took the position that a rail company was his business partner, transporting his product. He soon got to be one of the powerful in Kirchen County, but bigger powers and their secrets broke him down."

Nilda paused, wringing her hands in her lap. Then suddenly with both open hands she smacked the arms of her chair and resumed her story.

"I wasn't born yet. I was just a twinkle in my Mama and Papa's eyes then, as they say, when my folks came to Kirchen County and started farming and raising some livestock over by the North Dakota line. They came from Missouri. That's probably how we came by our Democratic leanings. Our ranch was about half way between the railroads, the C. M. Saint P and P to the south and the NP down to Beach and Glendive. It was dry land farm, and some just good for grass and sagebrush grazing.

"This was all before that night to put an end to the troubles. Our family changed after. The troubles didn't leave, they came to stir around in Papa's heart. Has Madge told you about the killing?"

"No more than you just did. Can you say more? Tell me about it."

"She'll have to tell you. I'm still not real sure where I stand with Madge. It's more than sixty years ago. I was young then. We both were. We get along now, I think—but I'm not certain about it. There's things we don't talk about, so I'm always a little nervous with Madge. There's still something about it. I don't know. She'll have to tell you. Then you can ask me again. Maybe I worry too much."

"Over and over the Bible says 'don't be afraid' or 'fear not'," I said. "Still we worry, don't we. Madge also mentioned something she called the League. Do you know anything about that?"

Nilda paused, kneading one hand with the other in her lap, staring down at them for nearly a minute before she replied, "That you'll have to study for yourself. Go to the library and look up the Nonpartisan League for yourself. And remember, I'm still a Democrat, but the way it really worked in Kirchen County back then wasn't like what you read about. The Great War showed us the worst of ourselves in a way."

I was hearing lots of story from the old days. And more was unsaid than said, it seemed.

We said our goodbyes, but not without a prayer. Madge didn't seem to care or notice whether the pastor prayed with her, but Nilda would always make sure we prayed together every time we met.

I wandered out to the sunshine after rain. With much to ponder from my visits, I walked the ten blocks home, forgetting that I had driven there during the rainstorm. The family car was still parked at Prairie Manor.

At home, the first thing I heard as I walked in the door was Berta calling from the back room, "I'm glad you're finally home. I need to run to the store."

Uh-oh. It was only then that I realized that I'd left the car. My confession didn't bring any sympathy. I was immediately sent to retrace my steps. Another dreamy, though hurried, walk time had me considering how my elderly friends kept sending me on missions—to an old homestead and into library research. It would be a search for the meaning of this event they call "the killing," along with something I'd never heard of that they called The Nonpartisan League. Nilda had also referred in passing to a war that must be World War I, which raised other questions for me. If I had been thinking that a killing was only in Madge's imagination, with Nilda's corroborating story I discarded that idea.

Then I spent the short drive home after my foolish forgetfulness worrying that Berta might actually be mad at me. She didn't find my offer to run the store errand helpful. She said she still needed a few minutes away from children before supper.

My worry was replaced by mild embarrassment. Berta and the girls were laughing about daddy the absent-minded professor when I walked in the door.

5

With local history questions swirling in my head, I had a hard time focusing on my next task of the week—preparing for a Sunday church service. Maybe our Community Church's 'Friday Men's Breakfast' group could help with both. The only thing I was certain about in that moment was that I didn't know enough yet to make helpful connections between text and town. "Text and town," I thought, "I'd better avoid using too much of that preacher talk. But saying Bible in one hand, newspaper in the other isn't less so." I couldn't yet make sense of Madge's and Nilda's stories to fit them into our larger faith story. It would not yet preach. Even so, I did see clearly that finding that fit was really what needed to happen if we were to understand our life story together.

Maybe the men could help. I tried to be the first to arrive at the Hilltop Café, a diner on the highway, actually at the bottom of a small hill. This time I found Chuck there waiting, his first time with the group since my arrival. He lived on a ranch forty-five miles out along unpaved roads. He greeted me by informing me that the day was half over. It wasn't yet 6:30 AM. Chuck said he'd already been to the elevator and sold a load of oats.

The guys were gathering before I could test my questions solo with Chuck. We ordered our breakfasts. Gary, our youngest member, a recent journalism graduate from North Dakota State didn't let us down. He shared his joke for the week, "Why are most North Dakota jokes so short?"

There were mumbles around the table and, "Why Gary?"

"So Montanans can remember them."

The mumbling became a groan chorus.

Then, as we were eating and visiting, according to our pattern, I interrupted our shooting-the-breeze by reading the Bible lesson that I intended to use for my sermon that week. I read in the New Testament from the letter to the Ephesians, including these verses (Ephesians 3:16-17):

> [I pray] that, according to the riches of his glory, he may grant you to be strengthened with might through his Spirit in the inner man (sic—I read it 'person'), and that Christ may dwell in your hearts through faith; that you, being rooted and grounded in love,...

Before anyone could respond, either with questions or thoughts from my reading, or, as often happened, by persistent return to the topics of their table talk that I'd interrupted, I repeated those words "rooted and grounded" and began to share a bit of what I was hearing about earlier times in Kirchen County and over in Sage County, North Dakota.

I did not bring up what Madge and Nilda had called "the killing." I thought that deep and nagging question too much for this day. I did ask about the League. I said it that way, and no one seemed to have any idea what the women had been referring to.

Chuck asked it this way: "The Major Leagues, the League of Women Voters—what?"

So I answered, "It was something actually called the Nonpartisan League." If there was any general knowledge about it, the table was surrounded by poker players. I looked at blank stares. No one seemed to have heard of it. Or at least no one would admit to any knowledge except, eventually, for Cal.

Cal considered himself a newcomer to Harstad, like me. It was the very first thing he told me when we met. Then I learned that he and his middle school teacher wife had been in town for at least six years. Cal's job was driving water truck in the oil patch, but he considered his vocation to be philosopher and scholar. He'd read all he could find of local history. While the other guys were silent Cal offered this observation, "If you really want to understand what's going on in this community, you need to learn about the Nonpartisan League, the grain merchants and the railroads in 1915, 1920 thereabouts."

All of us around the table were waiting for Cal to say more. He looked around at us with astonishment in his eyes that we could be so ignorant. We looked back, anticipating some explanation. Then Cal looked at his watch and stood up while saying, "Well, I've got to get to work." And turning to me he added, "Do like you said the old ladies told you. Read up on it." With that he paid for his eggs and headed for his pickup.

Gary, who'd been silently studying the poker faces, added simply, "Yup."

***

Our talk turned to geography. I sought help about locating that single section of land that had long ago been the Bowdler farm across the state line in Sage County. It had been nearly sixty years since the bank had foreclosed. Homesteads were 320 acres by then, and they had managed to double it. They claimed one in Elwin's name with another 320 adjoining acres in Madge's maiden name. Now it had been added among others to some larger holding. A farm and name in that other state at another time had the guys shaking their heads. Men who kept so much knowledge of who ranched where and for how long in their heads, seemed as surprised at their ignorance as I. I saw nods accepting what I could describe, but uncertainty about recognizing the actual place.

They had ideas about how to find the general area, but they were doubtful about my ability to spot the landmarks that Madge had described. I also hoped to find the Franks farm somewhere in Kirchen County, where Nilda lived as a child. Now more cattle ranch than wheat farm, the guys would be able to point it out on a county map, if we had one. Ed said, "Look on your farmstead map. Pastor Tim did leave that map at the parsonage for you, didn't he? It's now a piece of a McCracken spread, a section near the corner of the county."

Sally, our waitress, overheard a bit this talk as she topped up our coffee mugs. So she chimed in, "I lived right by Sage City until I was ten, back when it was a real town, probably six or eight hundred people right in the town when I was real little. I think those landmarks the old lady told you are still there to be found. You just keep your eyes peeled, Pastor. Don't let these guys scare you. Look for the wagon tracks—the grass'll be growing in ruts a wagon width apart. Don't just get to gazing across that big wide beautiful prairie out there or you'll miss it."

Ed took Sally's cue and got a litany of advice going, "You're not intending to go out Gilead Creek in that outfit you drive are you? What is that car?"

"It's a Renault 12. Hey, it's a good car.....at least three starts out of ten." I couldn't quite figure why my first reaction was to be defensive. We all knew it was junk, but with student loans to pay, all our family could afford at the time.

"You'll need something higher off the ground, something that starts when you turn the key. When are you planning to go out there? I might be able to let you use a pickup. I'll be cutting my irrigated hay all week, but Lois can set you up." This was Chuck being generous. Chuck and Lois lived nearly as far out, but in the opposite direction. The Renault would have as little chance of getting to their place and back.

Marion 'Sherm' Sherman lived and worked in town. His offer could be more helpful. "We'll be camping in the Long Pines over Labor Day, after that if you go out on Tuesday or Wednesday you can use my truck. It's a four-by-four, but you shouldn't need that."

It was unlikely, but I had to try, "You sure you want to trust me with that fine vehicle? How about it. You come along."

"Oh, I'd like to. But somebody has to mind the shop. With the work I got piled up I won't mind having the pickup gone for a day. That way nobody can call me away. They'll just have to wait."

"And it'll be my fault," I said. "Sounds great, I guess."

"You don't sound too excited about your little adventure," Gary said.

"Oh, I really want to get a look at these places. I do want to connect this history I'm learning about with the places," I said, a bit defensively. "But all those scoria and dirt back roads."

Ed grabbed a napkin and a pencil. His map will make it as clear as Powder River, which we all know is too thin to plow and too thick to drink. "Just head north out of town, take a right on Sage City Road. It's not very well marked. I think there's a little sign there somewhere. Anyway, if you pass the big overhead gate to the Sparkman Ranch you've gone about two miles too far. Turn east on Sage City. It goes straight as an arrow for about twenty miles. After it bends a little, about three or four miles further there'll be a fork. Take it." Ed waited, but nobody laughed. "Take the right fork, that's a little narrower than the left. The left is the main road heading to Sage, which is the only way I've ever taken out there. But I think where you want is more south toward some badlands. The place you're looking for has got to be this side of the badlands out there."

All the helpful advice made me more nervous. How many forks and crossroads will I see that Ed hasn't mentioned because they aren't the one he's visualizing and drawing on the napkin? Aloud, I said, "You know, I think I have a pretty good bump of direction....when there are mountains on the horizon. Out here, though, it's one dried up wheat field, sky, then another wheat field and more sky."

The time to wrap up our meeting arrived. As he pushed his chair back from the table, Sherm said, "Just come to the shop either Tuesday or Wednesday morning. We'll get you going. No mountains, but even out here, and in Dakota, too, the sun will be in the East in the morning, West in the afternoon. You shouldn't have a problem. You'll see the country, but probably not the remains of your dugout house. Worth a try, though."

It sounded like almost everyone would be in the Long Pines for the long weekend. And I still didn't even know where or what the Long Pines were.

6

Tuesday came. No point in putting it off any longer. I arrived at Sherm's machine shop at nine o'clock sharp and found him already well into his day's work. He reached over the workbench, grabbed keys from a pegboard hook and tossed them to me. Sherm quickly reconsidered that level of trust and followed me out to the big shiny white outfit. I climbed up behind the wheel as he instructed me about how to care for his special vehicle.

"That paper sack must be your lunch, huh. Got Ed's napkin map in there? It'll be good to wipe your hands, and not much more. Instead of that sandwich you might want to see if the café in Sage is open. Haven't been there for years, but they used to make a real nice hot hamburger. Give you a chance to ask how to find the places you still can't find after driving around all morning."

With those encouraging words, a real map, Sherm's water jug and my sack lunch I headed for the open country. It was a clear, crisp September morning. Autumn was upon us. I headed up the highway remembering Ed's directions as, "When you get to the Sparkman ranch, go back two miles, and head east." So, I drove slowly and looked for road markers. Sage City Road did have a sign, on a steel post bent almost parallel to the ground. Still, I wondered why Ed didn't mention the construction site of the new MDU natural gas pumping plant less than 300 yards before my turnoff.

Head straight east for about twenty miles, they said. It was perfectly straight and mostly flat; except for the washouts, holes and ruts in the scoria road, that is. All along the straight road were fields of after-the-meager-harvest stubble, golden brown over gently rolling hills. I passed a couple of abandoned farm houses and crumbling barns along the way, the straight-east way. A herd of a dozen antelope were feeding on the stubble. One field along the right side of the road had some green shoots under the stubble. Must be an early planting of winter wheat done no-till like the Conservation Service folks are promoting, helped by the recent rain. Maybe I had been paying more attention to the farmer talk around town than I realized.

Finally I came to an actual curve in the road. Was this the one? Such a gentle curve, not a right angle section corner. The land curved up and down just a bit more, too. Coming down a hill, a couple miles in the distance were some sandstone outcroppings, like a small version of the Medicine Rocks. And beyond that a stream bed, but I couldn't tell yet whether any water flowed. I drove on, watching for the fork. I wondered whether I'd yet crossed the state line. Madge had said it wasn't marked, but I hoped that had changed since she was last out here.

Then after driving over a cattle guard, quite suddenly the road became smoother. I decided that must be the state line and the NoDaks had actually graded it since last winter. The road wound along a border between open cropland on my left and rougher, badland kind of country carved by little Gilead Creek on my right. No sign of that fork in the road yet, but I stopped anyway to walk around a bit and take in the awesome, wide landscape around me. Drying stubble hid the small green shoots of new winter wheat. Turning to the right, the scene became strata of red clay, sandstone tan and lignite black in small canyons and stony pillars. The land dropped away down to the creek bed winding through on its way toward the Little

Missouri. The only water, puddles rippled by the breeze in shaded oxbows of the creek bottom, kept silent vigil waiting for winter snows and next spring's thaw to carry it north through the much larger badlands of TR Park and into the Big Missouri.

I went on my way again, up a gentle long slope. In not much more than a mile I came to the fork. I could hope. A rougher road, little more than wagon trail, wound off to the right, down along the badland to the creek, where it would wind into flatter country again at a somewhat lower elevation. There wasn't a bridge. The trail crossed the creek with a poured concrete ford, laid in shallow V, bone dry at the end of this droughty summer, in spite of recent rains. I thought to myself, "'crick' they call it. A better term might be 'arroyo', or better yet, to go with its name from the Hebrew Scripture, call this 'Wadi Gilead'." Wet in springtime, mud in early summer, dust until autumn rains—if they come. About a hundred yards up the creek was a grove of cottonwoods. I gazed that direction, not really seeing until a large bird flapped from the ground to a low cottonwood branch. Looking closer, seeing that there were several of them, I wondered, "Are those birds really what they look like? Are those wild turkeys?"

The track ran up a gentle slope on the other side, more or less following along a ridge above a creek. I had a feeling that I was going up an even smaller streambed, no longer down toward the Little Missouri. The path took me a little farther away from the stream, and then I saw it. There was an earthen dam, standing high and dry at first glance. And an old, long unused track beyond a fence line. I shut off the pickup, parked in the middle of the path. I had seen no one since I left the paved highway north of Harstad. Still, out of long habit, I pulled the key.

The day was getting quite warm. I shucked my jacket, tossed it on the seat, took a long drink of water from the two gallon Coleman jug that Sherm had pushed into the cab after he saw that I had no more liquid than fit in my brown lunch bag. Harstad town well water, but I was thirsty enough to drink it, alkali and all, anyway.

An hour earlier I had watched antelope dive under the low strand of a barbed wire fence. So I was determined to use their technique. Until I got to the fence. Instead, I pushed the strand up while I crawled, I thought low enough, but still snagged and tore my t-shirt. After a grumbled word people think pastors don't use, I added, still out loud, "Oh well, I won't be in too much trouble at home, once I explain that it could easily have been my new jacket."

Once I'd taken a few steps from the fence line and down the path I could see that there was some water low in the dam. Since I am not a ranch guy, I was relieved to see that there weren't any cattle drinking there, or anywhere in sight. Why do I never remember to carry a camera?

I followed the path, nearly lost in the wheatgrass and sage. All around, silver sage dotted the uncultivated bits of prairie in its late summer yellow bloom. Could this be the place that Madge called the prettiest farm you ever did see? I walked around and examined the area, over cut bank and rocky outcropping. I would have something to report to Madge at our next visit.

***

Back at the pickup I realized that my wandering about had taken longer than I thought possible. The sun was high in the sky, a few distant storm clouds were beginning to appear on the north horizon.

Before the day was over I still hoped that I might find the place that the Franks family ranched, where Nilda spent her early childhood. With new confidence that I wasn't going to get permanently lost, I figured I might head home by way of section line roads. Once back in Montana I could make use of my Kirchen County farmstead map, if I could figure out where I would be crossing the state line. I backtracked to the fork and, on a whim, turned right, toward Sage City, following "Wadi" Gilead downstream. Might as well get a look at what's left of Sage City, maybe get a café lunch, and advice about back roads.

Within a mile or two the road was no longer the border between badland country and farm. Now it was low hills, alternatively dry land strip farm, pastures of grazing cattle, and irrigated alfalfa in the lowlands near the streams. A baler was working at the far end of one of these fields of windrowed hay, making those huge new bales that require machinery to lift.

At the next rise grain elevators that must be Sage City appeared in the distance. I pulled into town slowing to a crawl. The café looked permanently closed, as did most of main street. The railroad spur line was just a flat trail. I could see where the tracks had been until fairly recently. By the look of the elevator the last train had come and gone a long time ago. The corrugated sheet metal siding was peeling away from the rough planks wherever the wind could catch it. Between the rail bed and main street was a little park with a rough picnic table and a few cottonwoods, almost in the shadow of the elevator. It was there that I ate my sack lunch of a bologna sandwich, apple, a can of pop and a handful of Oreos. I looked around at a ghost town where, by the appearance of occupied houses, as many as a hundred people still lived. Houses looked lived-in but nothing larger than grasshoppers stirred.

It was time to head for home, or look for the Franks Ranch. The county road looked to be paved. I could take it south and go home on blacktop. Or, take the county road for a ways and turn west on the next section line road, take a look around and still be home when the neighbor kids get out of school, or soon after. But not very likely before Ruthie's kindergarten dismissal time. Either direction, I'd start the same, so it was time to fold up the maps and get going.

Preoccupied with the folding and daydreaming, I didn't hear him approach until the gears were grinding behind me and an ancient Chevy pickup truck drifted to a stop alongside the elevator. The driver's door opened with a long squeak of creaking hinges and a sun and wind weathered face, shaded by a wide-brimmed hat, appeared over the top of the cab. The cowboy called out. I wandered over as he jumped down from the running board and leaned on the side of the truck box, watching me. As I got closer it looked like he and his truck matched in their weather beaten aging. I rested my arms on the box opposite him. Scattered in the truck box were tools of his trade, a saddle and tack (but no horse), long handled shovel, large coils of wire, two come-alongs, and a rusty tool box. Scattered among the tools were dozens of empty Grain Belt Beer cans. Like the tools, he was rusted, too. His gray hair hung in a tangled mass behind a three day beard of white whiskers. He could have been anywhere from sixty to ninety years old.

I greeted him, glad of the first human contact since I left Harstad hours earlier, "Almost a summer day today, isn't it."

"It'll be cold soon enough. Are you lost, friend? Or did you steal Sherm's high class outfit and you're looking for a place to hide?"

"Not lost...at least not yet. I'm trying to use some back roads without getting lost, get a look at the country, get in touch with some history of the area around here. Sherm loaned me his fancy F-150 because he didn't want me broken down out here in my unreliable car. Guess I better not get lost or he will report it stolen. So you're a friend of Sherm's?"

"Some history?" That part seemed to intrigue him. And he obviously didn't want to answer the friend question. We introduced ourselves. He gave his name, something mumbled into his hat, and asked what I did. My reply explained the soft hands he'd been giving a critical eye.

He came back to the history question that I answered, "Yes. I'm told that the place I'm looking for next is now a section of McCracken property over in Montana, in the corner of Kirchen County. So, I thought I'd drive south look for a section line road going west, see where it leads."

"McCracken, eh. I worked for that outfit for a while. Few years back. Did your friends say which corner of the county? McCracken covers his bets, you know. Has acreage here and there. If one spread gets hailed out, he figures to get a crop somewhere else."

"Well, I'm looking for the place where the Franks family had a homestead in 1915 or so."

"They must've lost it a long time back. That name doesn't ring a bell. I'm real old, lived out here a long time, but I didn't grow up here. If you take the, let's see, (the motion of his fingers marked the counting on the picture in his head) the fifth or sixth section line road after the pavement ends, it'll take you past McCracken's north property. You'll turn a couple corners before you get into Montana, though. 'Course the land doesn't look much different than what you see right from here."

At that I interrupted, "Hey, you could do better at tourist promotion than that. Locals are supposed to pretend it doesn't all look the same. And, you know, when I look close, there are differences that surprise me."

"Yeah, I suppose. But when you spend the whole of July stringing fence wire out here, it's just miles and the come-along pulls just as hard on the top strand as on the bottom."

I half expected to hear him use Madge's matter-of-fact statement, "I've seen wet and I've seen dry."

Instead, he continued, "You come tourist-like, looking for the history. Somebody does that, asking about folks in 1915 and so on, I worry they're looking for information about A.C. Townley. If that's your cause, just go the hell on down to Beach and let me be."

"Townley?" I asked, "Who was Townley to get you riled up? What about 1915 makes you come up with that name?"

"Aw shit, did I say that name? You never heard it from me, and don't say you did."

I preferred to leave on friendly terms, so I let it go and started to express my thanks. Next I figured to head toward Montana and home.

Before I could go, there had to be more navigation advice, though. "Now, if the spread you're looking for is that other corner, and you want to find it from here, you'll be going about forty miles south, twisting through some good badlands. Take the main highway into Montana and go another twenty south on an unpaved state road. And if you come to a gate that says Pearson Ranch, you've gone too far and you'll run out of road."

I was dutifully taking this all in. Those guys at breakfast knew all this, and still didn't specify which corner of the county. It was obvious that the south end would be too much for this day, so I hadn't tried to follow those directions very closely. And Nilda had said something (what was it?) that made me think it must be at the north end. I thanked Mr. Mumble-into-hat, and headed for the borrowed, not stolen, pickup. Back in the oversized cab, I took another look at my Kirchen County farmstead map. There it was, down near the southeast corner, another three sections labeled McCracken, and Pearson south of that.

So, I headed out ready to count the section roads as soon as the surface turned from blacktop to red scoria. I'd been touring long enough by this time that the fields, fence lines, and straight roads did all look the same. Now there was another research question to track down. Who was A.C. Townley?

I counted, took some turns – all section corner, never by a curve of the road – and eventually knew where I was. The blacktop and US highway sign pointed me toward home, still uncertain whether I'd even taken a look at the place I intended to visit, not even knowing in which corner of the county to look. The highway signs assured me that somewhere out there I had traveled from North Dakota section lines to Montana back roads, and I could hardly tell any difference.

***

So many questions bounced around in my little mind. The library should be my next stop. But, of course, I did have my vocation as pastor to attend to, and I was still a beginner at that job, too. And visits to Prairie Manor really counted as part of the day job. The library will be there. By the time I get there, no doubt, there will be a longer list of names and references to look up.

Back in Harstad, I topped up the tank and returned Sherm's pickup. He jokingly expressed gratitude for the North Dakota dirt I'd imported on the sides of the vehicle that had been shiny white in the morning. Was I supposed to have left the dust in a car wash drain? This Eastern Montana culture of understatement can be so confusing.

As soon as I walked in the door at home a message was passed along. Ruthie said, "You're supposed to bring the song books, Daddy." Berta clarified the message, "Rachel called a little while ago. She asked if you'd bring the box of song books from the church with you to the Manor? I had to tell her where you'd gone and that we expected you back soon."

I'd forgotten my Tuesday obligation. It wasn't yet too late, but almost. With no time for a thorough clean up from my dusty day, I'd be visiting Prairie Manor sooner than expected.

7

Nilda was chatting with a couple of the singers as they waited for the song books and our leader to arrive. I saw no sign of Madge, though. I had no chance to look for her. Rachel came rushing in, anxious to get started before the bustle of dinner trays would end our concert time.

After the singing, Nilda was glad to hear that I was getting acquainted with the rural areas. She assured me that I had visited the right part of the county. "It's sad that the old place is just a piece of a field for the giant tractors to plow across," she said. "We had a good little place there. My brothers worked in the fields with Papa and mostly without him....after."

It looked like I was in for a long story. Then her supper tray arrived, drawing her attention to the meal. So she left me with just a tease of something and I was able to excuse myself. I was anxious to get home to my own supper and family, but I needed to check on Madge.

I found her sitting in her room. "I'm feeling some better now," she said. "I felt so poorly this morning that I just laid myself down in bed for most of the day. Oh, I'll be alright though."

I just wished her well. This time we had a short prayer together. I said I'd be back in a couple days to tell her about my adventures in Sage County. Her brief illness had me feeling a mixture of concern for my elderly friends, along with a more self-interested urgency that I get the whole story while she can still tell it.

8

The coming of fall meant my week was suddenly filled with more scheduled programs and expectations on my time. The Friday breakfast was still one of those expectations. On this occasion only Gary, Sherm and I were on hand. My talk about the fun I had touring the region led to general conversation about our dry year, the difficulties farmers were facing, and appreciation for our open spaces, but not to my history questions.

That afternoon, however, I finally found enough time to visit at the Manor when I wouldn't be looking at my wristwatch repeatedly. I had a story to tell that I really hoped would encourage Madge and Nilda to trust enough to tell me theirs. I may have been unskilled at pastoral counseling, but I could see that there were events in the stories of struggle and conflict that ought not continue to be hidden just under the surface as they seemed to be.

On the way up to the Manor entry I nearly walked past Madge without seeing her. She was sitting in a wheelchair on the front patio visiting with a couple other manor residents. She saw me and called a greeting. Madge began to introduce me to the others, then checked herself. To me she asked, "You're the pastor, right?"

I nodded assent and answered, "Yes. That's right. I'm Pastor Wil."

Then she turned and pointed toward her friends, "Pastor, this is.." She paused and her friends told me their own names. Then they both left us, claiming to feel a bit chilly.

"How about you, Madge? Are you ready to go inside?"

As she tucked the afghan blanket more tightly around her legs, Madge said, "No. It's nice out here. Oh, I do love this time of year. And I've seen a lot of them. I'm the oldest, you know. The ash and aspen trees and cottonwoods in the gullies turn color. The harvest is in, maybe taken to market. If it was a good harvest, we'd know if "big biz" was cheating us too bad to meet the mortgage in spite of our good work. Oh, by the way, did you go look at our pretty place yet?"

"Yes, I did. And I drove along the section lines. It looked to me like most places out there had some grain to harvest in spite of how dry it's been. I drove down through some badland country, talked to a real live working cowboy at Sage City. He looked like he might've started as a drover before they fenced the range. Now he mostly mends fence."

"Old like me and still working, huh. Well, bless his fool heart."

"Anyway, Madge, what I wanted to tell you—I think I found your homestead. I was sure surprised I could. It turns out that your directions and description were really good. It is fenced all across there, but I could see the berm of the dam from the road. There isn't much water in the dam, but there's some, a puddle way down the bank. No cattle anywhere to be seen, and I'm just as glad of that. I could relax and wander around, see if I was in the right place without thinking about a herd of big animals nearby. I'm just not a ranch kid, I guess."

Madge was quietly chuckling, almost under her breath, as I made that admission. I let her enjoy the moment, then continued, "I walked from the dam up along the cut bank, looking for any sign of the sod and dugout house you described.

All of a sudden I saw where it was, and I was practically standing in the middle of it. Was it really that small?"

"Yep."

"And you had how many children there?"

"Five. But they were small, too. What am I saying? There were never seven of us in that little dugout. We had the frame house by the time Peter was born. It just felt like more in that tiny cabin. On a winter evening we'd be packed in there so tight the mice had to wait in the snow outside the door. We were what you might call a close-knit family, in more ways than one."

And Madge was still smiling at her cleverness as the tears began to well in her eyes. Looking wistfully at nothing she paused. Then before I could go on with my report, she continued. "We built the house then, hardly got well settled in it before Elwin was gone from us. I knew you couldn't find where it was, because it got moved off the land. Where it was is all plowed ground now."

The sun moving across the sky left us in the building's shade. I could see that Madge was beginning to get cold. Still, it was she who suggested it. "Let's go inside, now, and you can tell me all about your exploring."

We wheeled to the sunny corner of the big room. Madge was content to stay in the new wheelchair so I sat in her favorite comfy chair. That put us at eye level with neither of us having to look up or down, which let us converse comfortably. I wanted to tell about my discoveries....until she mentioned losing Elwin. Then I wanted to hear more of what that was about. Still, Madge was the oldest and she would always set our agenda. "Tell me about your travels, now, Pastor."

"Well, like I said, I was standing in the middle of a flat, grassy spot along the cut bank when I realized I was in the middle of your dugout house. When I looked around, there were even some rotting timbers up on the bank that must have been part of the sod roof." She nodded an unspoken urge that I go on.

"Looking down at the cut bank from the ridge, I noticed something sticking out of the dirt where your dugout back wall would have been. Look what I found." I handed her an age-blackened tin spoon, with its handle bent into a backward loop.

Now Madge was really getting weepy as she marveled, "Well, look at that. It's Pearl's baby spoon. Oh my, you've made my day, Pastor. She'll be so surprised. She's retired to Arizona, but she calls me every week. I can't wait to tell her."

With that Madge quieted again. She had set our agenda, and my story was to come first today, so I continued. "I wandered further along the cut bank ridge, up a little knob hill over a little sandstone cliff. I was looking around, enjoying the view across the wide prairie. But I did look around for what I might see on the ground, too. And eventually I came across another old, worn plank of wood. I thought at first it might be part of the outhouse, but there weren't any other boards out there at all. So, I took a closer look. There's some faded writing on it that I couldn't make out at all. It could say Elwin Bowdler, or it might just say Fels Naptha Soap for all I know. Anyway, I decided it must be the grave marker, so I dug a little bit with my hands. I didn't even have a pocket knife on me, and I didn't want to use the little spoon I'd just found. So, I dug with my hands enough to set the plank upright with some soil banked and stones against it, said a short prayer, and headed back to the road. I'd agree with you that it's a real pretty place if only there were some Rocky Mountains to look at on the horizon."

Now, finally, it was Madge's turn to reminisce. "You and your mountains. Just block the view, I say. But Pastor, I am so pleased you found the old place, and put Elwin's marker upright. Some things I remember, some I don't. For all I know that grave marker might've said R.I.P on one side and soap on the other."

"You're a wry wit, you know that Madge?"

"Pshaw. No Pastor Wil, I'm just an old lady who's been blessed to live through changing times, different worlds on nearly the same patch of ground. One of those was that pretty little farmyard, with the kiddies running or toddling around me, a wash tub and clothes line, wood stove and a little garden. And a good man who thought he could help Mr. Townley and the League make things better for the farmers of North Dakota."

"Townley, you say. You know, Madge, the man I met in Sage City mentioned that name. More like he spat it. He said people snooping around for history out there were always wanting to learn about A.C. Townley. Then he wanted me to forget he'd mentioned the name. Real hateful about that subject and real friendly otherwise. Townley's connected to the Nonpartisan League then? What is it about this Townley guy and your League? These people and things that I'd never heard of before?"

"Oh, I expect your cowboy friend heard just enough when he was growing up that now he thinks he can blame Townley and the League for everything from the times when communists could get elected up north to the troubles farmers are having now. I might be cooped up in this so-called rest home, but I notice things. And even I can see that the cause of trouble now is the same as what the League fought against. And we made things better for a bit, before the war stirred up the other troubles."

Madge was making her point of view more plain, and hinting at more to come, but now she was getting that faraway look in her eyes again. I had to resist the urge, as always, to push another question on her. I was learning how futile that could be. I would have to let the story come as she would tell it.

After what felt like several minutes, but was probably much less, Madge spoke again. "I kept a good garden at that place on Gilead Creek. Maybe if there was still that garden with the corn taller than you and beans climbing the poles I set. It was between the house and the dam, all fenced but the deer and the birds helped themselves anyway. Maybe if you could've seen that, you wouldn't need those dang mountains to understand how pretty a farmstead could be. All the long winter I'd be dreaming what I'd plant, and how I could make it better than last year. When spring finally came Elwin would plow it over for me before he even planted the alfalfa and spring wheat.

That's only if the winter wheat wasn't coming up. I might even plant something new, ordered from the seed catalog, but mostly it was seeds from last year, and from trades with the neighbors.

"I had two tin boxes I kept up on the shelf. One was for the seeds to plant in spring, that I hoped would sprout. The other was where I put the egg money. Where I saved for the seed order, if it didn't have to go for something else first. It most often did. Eggs never really made us any real money, but it helped. When I had some extra eggs or fresh cream, it'd be an excuse to make Elwin haul us all to town with him. He'd make a fuss about the extra work taking us all on the wagon, and the extra time it'll take in town. We never had a tin lizzie. Elwin was still hoping to drive a League organizer's Model T when he got killed. We'd pile onto that old wagon and be on the way. All his complaining stopped just as soon as the horses stepped into that slow walking pace he'd allow them, so we didn't bounce around on the rough track. He'd make the ride such a happy time, singing with the kiddies, pointing out all the different plants and weeds. He could name most all of them and he'd be teaching about the weeds that could cause the most trouble in the crops and what made good range for cattle. He was a smart farmer, called himself a scientific farmer, self-schooled. Here he'd started out the morning grumping about how we'd take too much time, and then we'd get all our town business and visiting over with and wait for Elwin who'd still be swapping lies with all the other farmers there for market day.

"For visiting on market day in Sage City you had to understand speaking broken—broken English, broken Norwegian, broken German that had some broken Russian mixed in with it. And Elwin could handle it. We weren't immigrants ourselves, you understand. We came from Wisconsin, but the same languages were around us there, too. The lumberjacks there in the north woods came from all over. And Elwin's family were the sort that got along with everybody. I was so blessed to marry into that clan. But they were not a bit clannish, is what I'm saying to you. I wasn't so sure about it when Elwin got the itch to move west. But those posters and pamphlets from the rail companies made it look so fine.

"Anyway, where was I? Oh yes, meanwhile, back at the ranch, as they say. One year I was able to keep more laying hens than my usual, and we had more garden produce than I needed to can. That was '15 I believe, or '16. I didn't get a good price, but I sold eggs and carrots and squash and cream through that early fall. I saved up the coins in my tin box. Then a man driving a nearly new Model T Ford came calling. Said he wanted to talk to Elwin about a new organization of farmers. He told how together we'd be able to get control of things in North Dakota and not be beholden all the time to whatever the big biz guys decide. He said that a lot: big biz this, big biz that. Sounded to me like he might be trying to start his own big biz by swindling us. But the more he talked, the more it started making sense. I could tell that Elwin's mind was going a mile a minute there that night in the kitchen at our new frame house. We were struggling, you see. That house meant that we didn't just borrow for the next crop, now the bank had a big lien on the whole property just so we could live in a house and not a hole in the ground."

As she paused for a moment a nurse's aide approached Madge and me. "I'm sorry to interrupt, sir. But Madge, it's time to get ready for supper. We need to take care of some things at your room first, remember."

I was sorry she had to interrupt, too, until I realized how long we'd been talking, first outside, then in the corner of the favorite chair that the afternoon sun had by now abandoned. I headed for home and supper marveling at the memories Madge had to share, and realizing that I would have to come another day to visit with Nilda.

***

Although it was still a little earlier than our usual suppertime, I found everyone in the kitchen preparing. Ruthie was setting plates around the table, Rebecca, our three year old, was folding napkins as Roberta added macaroni to boiling water. Mmm, mac and cheese and hot dogs. Becca announced, "We're going to the football, daddy, and you're coming, too,."

"Is that right? And I'm invited," I said, looking to Berta to fill me in.

She did, saying, "Mary Ann suggested it. She said she'd help keep track of the girls. Even said that if it gets cold, or the kids get bored, that she'd be happy to leave early with them. If we need to, Mary Ann and I can both see to the kids. The weather is mild. It's the first home game, so I think we should go."

We couldn't ask for better next door neighbors than Mary Ann and Henry. It would even be good for me to be at the game in support of our high school kids. The macaroni was ready now, so we all sat down. I turned the conversation to my afternoon visit with Madge.

"Madge told a long story today, about her life before the killing. She still won't talk about what that was, except that it's clear that it was her husband who was killed. Everything she tells hinges on it. The other day she told about times after, today we talked about before. I told her about seeing her homestead."

"What's a homestead? Can I see it, daddy?" Becca asked.

"You know, we should all go out that way one day," I replied. "But I can't say when. The breakfast guys are probably right when they say I shouldn't drive the Renault out there."

Berta asked, "How long are you going to let Madge mention 'the killing' and still skirt around ever talking about it?"

"I thought you said I shouldn't even get into the subject at all," I countered.

"Well, now that you are into the subject, why can't you just ask?"

"You should see how Madge holds tight to whatever agenda she has for the day. She will not be steered at all. So, I just listen and nod."

"Daddy, what's a homestead?" Becca persisted. Becca sticks to her agenda as firmly as Madge.

"Becca, a homestead was a way the government gave people some land if they would make it a farm to grow things for food," I answered. "The one I went to see is a farm that took me about two hours to get to in Mr. Sherman's truck."

Ruthie had been unusually quiet through these dialogues. Now she found an opening for her topic. "Will there be cheerleaders?"

"What? At a homestead?" I said with a start. "Oh....yes. There will. Right now I need to take a few minutes before we go to write in my journal about what I heard today. Okay?"

"Okay, daddy," Ruthie said. "Can we sit by the cheerleaders?"

I let Berta handle that one, and headed to the basement and my journal.

The day ended with a Harstad High victory, 13-7. Henry and I saw the second half while at her home, Mary Ann served warm cocoa to Berta and the girls.

9

The following Tuesday I went to Prairie Manor an hour before the time our singing group would gather. This would give plenty of time to visit with Nilda, and perhaps others. The door to her room was wide open. I knocked anyway. I found her wearing a long coat with purse in hand as if she were about to go out. Would this be another badly timed drop-in?

She quickly explained, "I'm just back from dinner with my daughter. My afternoon rest will just have to wait a little longer now, won't it. Please. Sit."

Her single room had two chairs. Both had been around a long time, and probably came from her home. One was a low dark green overstuffed chair, the other a bleached oak arm chair with padded seat from a dining set. I wanted Nilda to sit first because I wasn't sure which chair she preferred. After some more bumbling and helping her with her coat, I asked, "Which chair do you like?" She answered by easing herself all the way down into the low chair that sank even lower than it first appeared because the springs were giving out under her ample weight.

I sat facing a window at the front side of the Manor. I found myself gazing out where children were gathering on the play equipment in the park across the street. I thought, "School's out. Time for the kids to enjoy some outdoor play on a fall afternoon." I was about to start by telling Nilda about my search for her family's home of sixty plus years ago, though there really wasn't much to tell. Watching the kids play, my thoughts turned to wondering about what it was like for children on the farmstead when Nilda was young.

Nilda, following my eyes, turned to watch the children, too. "I'm privileged to have a room on this side where I can see the park. Have I met your children, Pastor?"

"I don't know. The girls are just five and three, so you may have heard their noisy disruptions during church. You were out with your daughter. And pictures on the bureau tell me you must have grandchildren. Do you have other children?"

"It's my daughter Magda who lives here. She has one son. His family are in Billings, so they're not so far away. My son is at Minot. Might as well be Siberia for all I hear from him. Last I knew his kids' families were strung out from California to Nebraska. But Pastor, you're not telling what you found on your little drive the other day."

"Okay. Well, first I made a beeline for North Dakota. And I found the homestead that Madge described to me. I found where their sod house had been dug out of the cut bank, the dam they had on the little creek there, and even what might have been her first husband's grave."

At the mention of the grave, Nilda stiffened, her expression visibly changed and she said through tight lips, "But tell me what you found of our Franks family ranch. I haven't been out that way for so many years I almost can't remember it."

I was thinking, "Can't remember? How can she not remember the home of her childhood when her memory seems so surprisingly sharp otherwise? What did the mention of Elwin's grave mean, that caused her to stiffen so?" What I said to her was, "I had learned that your family place is now part of McCracken's big holdings. Your ranch was in a corner of the county. Did you tell me that, or did I get that somewhere else? Anyway, I'd found the name McCracken on the county map and quit looking further. It had to be pointed out to me that

McCracken farms and ranches include acreage in both the northeast and southeast corners and more. So, I drove toward home by the shortest way that might take me past your spread. So, I'm not too sure if I found it or not. I did see some big wide country. And the fields are looking better after the rain last week. Winter wheat is sprouting. After such a dry summer the little bit of green is just amazing. And the sagebrush with the yellow flowers! I never noticed that before. Tell me about the homestead. Were you born there? When did your family leave the place?"

"Slow down, Pastor. I'm just taking in the scene you were telling about. Too many questions, but I'll try. My brothers and I were all born before Papa got the idea to sell out the farm near Gainesville. That's in Missouri, and Papa sold to the mining company. He sold before they pushed us out. They were ready to condemn our little acreage to pile the zinc mine tailings. Gramp and Gram had that farm before us, and I think maybe it was in the family even before them. I came out here when I was a little girl. I can remember the train ride, but I was little. It was exciting, coming to this new land. This was before Harstad was even a town, nor Kirchen even a county. Papa hauled the grain to Beach in those early days, so he kept up with the news in both states.

"Papa must have had some special knack, or maybe special knowledge that we never heard, that convinced the elevator man down there to grade our wheat honestly. As I was growing up I'd hear the men talk. They'd be complaining about how the shippers and millers all found ways to get a bigger cut and leave the farmer with nothing. I'd see Papa just listen and nod, and never say a word one way or the other. It was about the time I was getting engaged, fixing to marry Walter Ruud, I was. That's about when we started hearing this talk about the Nonpartisan League over in North Dakota. It wasn't mentioned much in Montana at all, except when somebody would scorn them for being socialists. Papa worried that it was just one more way the farmers would get the short straw again. The dues did seem awful high. They wanted $16.00 a year, even if it had to be paid with a check postdated to after harvest. Anyway,

49

Walt came on as Papa's hired hand. Supposed to be just for the season, but something else happened."

Nilda winked an eye, which I took to mean there were things between young lovers that would not be related to the pastor.

"I was back living in the farmhouse with Papa and Mom when Walt went to war. Magda was on the way, and got born. After the war Walt was different. Had a sad way about him. He didn't want to do farm work anymore. Just as well, since it couldn't really support that many. The farm and ranch stayed in the family though, nearly all through the Depression years. When Papa died young in '28 my brothers were already running it, and adding acreage from sheriff sales. Papa had been poorly for his last decade. I put it to that night in the summer of 1918. I believe that night broke him down. Walt and Papa, my men both broke down somehow."

Just then we heard the sounds of the piano and of more chatter in the hallway, of gathering people together for the Tuesday songs before supper. A conversation was once again ended with new questions. It was expected that I be with the group beside the piano already, but instead of hurrying on, I walked slowly to the dining and gathering room at Nilda's cane assisted pace. We walked in silence most of the way. Then, as we neared the seat at her assigned supper table, she took hold of my arm and looking more at the floor than at me, she asked, "Do I still have to carry the burden of that night? Does Papa's burden really have to be mine to carry, too? How could I have stopped it?"

I knew too little of the circumstance behind her questions to have an answer for her, but I couldn't just walk away with the questions hanging between us. I did what I could, and that was too little. I murmured, "I don't think so," looked at my watch and dashed for the singing group. At her room we had overlooked our usual closing prayer in our rush to the entertainment. Her pain-filled question came as a sort of incomplete prayer. Too much was still left unsaid. Too much was left unprayed.

10

With more new questions it was time to visit our local library. I needed some research with objectivity about the Nonpartisan League. I needed to find out what I could about a long ago violent death: "The killing." Are they talking about a murder, a tragic accident, or what? What facts might there be to help explain the grief and guilt still being both expressed and suppressed?

My only previous visits to the library had been a couple of times with the kids for Thursday story hour. So far my acquaintance was only the children's section. The library occupied a foyer, office and three classrooms on the ground floor of a former school building. The spacious area could hold much more than the modest collection of books on hand. I came early on Monday at what I hoped would be a slow time. It was.

Sophie Kettle, our town librarian, had come to Harstad just a few months before my family's arrival. She was making an special effort to prove to the community that she was worth the extra cost to have a qualified person with a degree in library science running things. She had told me about the skeptics who questioned the additional cost of her modest salary, how she had to prove herself, and even sought my support the first time we met at the Community Church. As she demonstrated her organization skills, she was already developing more clearly defined access to topics of local interest. So far, however, that area felt like an annex of a county agriculture extension office: gardening tips for our arid, alkali country, and so on. My questions would give her an excuse to make discoveries about local history and add to the library's resources.

As I came through the front door it banged shut, as it always did, with a noise to destroy forever the myth of the silent library. Sophie looked up from her work at the front counter checking in the returned books, getting them ready for re-shelving. Shorter than five feet, she almost had to look up to see over the counter. Her joke that she was not over weight, just under height actually rang true in her case.

As she greeted me with "Good morning, Reverend," her smile reached her deep brown eyes. "Looks like you're on your own today. No kids in tow?"

I think my face must have shown my discomfort with the appellation 'reverend'. I thought I was letting it pass as I said, "Not today, Sophie. Looks like you're on our own, too. No helpers at opening hour, I see. I've only come at story time, so I expect to find a boisterous crowd and volunteer helpers here."

"It is only me on the slow mornings," she said. "I like these quiet times with just one or two visitors around almost as much as I like the library full of children. Anyway, how can I help you?"

"I'm looking for information about some local history. A couple of our friends over at Prairie Manor have been telling me about their lives in homesteader days. They talk about something they call The League. When I mentioned that at the men's breakfast Cal said that if I want to understand the culture in Kirchen County I have to learn about the Nonpartisan League. So that's one question."

I continued with a digression, "Have you got acquainted with Cal? Lived here for years, but still thinks he's a newcomer. And he's probably right."

"Oh yes, I know Cal. He's one of our best interlibrary loan patrons. Interesting guy. My daughter is in his wife Jeanine's science class at the middle school. I think Jeanine is about the best teacher Stephanie's ever had. Not two weeks into the school year and she's already learning how to think like a scientist in Jeanine's class. Which reminds me, Rev—I was going to call you. Before you get away I have a couple questions for you, too."

"Ask away."

"Not yet. We'll get to that. But you came to learn about a nonpartisan league. Was that a real organization back then? Something local, maybe? I'm from Oregon and I've never heard of it."

"I believe it was. And I think it was mostly over in North Dakota. So my questions are local not just for Harstad, but also Sage County. Our Prairie Manor ladies, Madge and Nilda, have also mentioned a killing. That's how they refer to it, especially Madge. Nilda made mention of "that night" that changed her father, like there's a connection. But like the League, as soon as they mention these things, next they change the subject. And I've learned that it is best just to let them. If there are newspapers from 1918 and around that time, that'll probably be the only record of a murder or fatal accident."

Sophie sent me to the card catalog while she looked for whatever she might find among the filing cabinets and the catalog of microfilm records. I found a book listed: *Political Prairie Fire*, by Robert Morlan. So I headed to the stacks but did not find the book. Sophie was coming from the row of metal cabinets that librarians call the vertical file. She was shaking her head as she met me at the desk. She had found a reference to Senator Burton K. Wheeler's first run for office. It was under the Nonpartisan League banner. That might lead me to more in books of Montana history. I reported that the book in the card file seemed to be out. Sophie did a little checking on that and discovered that it had been discarded at least five years earlier. That the card hadn't been removed offended her meticulous librarian sensibilities, so she went immediately to the catalog, pulled the subject card, checked to make sure the author and title cards had been removed, then came back with an offer. Sophie said the Harstad Library isn't quite up with the latest technology, and the easiest way for her to get the book through interlibrary loan would be to make a few calls to other libraries. She would get on the phone as time allowed that day.

Then we turned to my question about a killing. I didn't really know enough specifics yet to begin the search. And Sophie let me know that there would be little to find at our library, "It won't surprise you to know, Rev, that the local history I studied as soon as I started here would be about the library itself. And the first public library didn't open until 1928. It was a volunteer effort, mostly wives of businessmen, with most of the books donated from the local readers—the 'literati'?—of Kirchen County."

I interrupted, saying, "The literati of Kirchen County. Now there's a concept to give one pause."

"Careful, Rev," she said. "You'd be amazed at the tomes your farm and ranch folk read and discuss during the long winter. Anyway, I was saying, the original library was housed in the front parlor of the doctor's big house, which was also his office waiting room. The volunteers got their own space a couple years later when two churches joined together into your Community Church. The little Brethren Church building became the library. That's more than you need to know. I tell it because it's my little corner of the world so I find it fascinating, and just to say there won't be much here about those earlier years. There wasn't any attempt to store newspapers and local reports until the 1940's. There won't be anything to find either on paper or microfilm, probably nothing closer than the state historical libraries in Helena and Bismarck."

"Well, I guess that's it for today, then," I replied, "but it is a start. I hope you can find that book. Guess I better get going."

"Just a minute, Rev. I still have a question for you, remember."

"Ah, yes. Now I can say it—ask away."

"I know you haven't seen us on Sunday very often. Maybe you'll see us more now that we're getting into the fall routine, and more settled in the community. Steph is making more friends now. But here's the situation. It's hard for a single mom in this town, and in the church it's even harder. I doubt there's much you can do about that, but I want you to know."

She was right of course. I could understand reasons for that discomfort, and I had no idea how it might be changed.

Sophie went on, "The other thing is this. What church programs are there for the teenage kids?"

"Oh, good. At least I have an answer for one thing, Sophie. Some high school and middle school kids are planning to meet this coming Sunday evening. We have a couple of take-charge sophomores who are pushing for a youth group themselves. So, I'm hopeful about that. I hope Stephanie will come, too. Six o'clock Sunday in the church basement. My agenda for the kids is to find some adults to help guide the group. Hint, hint."

"Oh, no. Don't push your luck, Rev."

"The other problem is beyond me, right now. I'm still feeling my way here, but I get the impression sometimes that while it's 1981 other places, but still '55 here. But I can't say that out loud, can I."

"Well, anyway, I'll try to get Steph there Sunday night," Sophie said. "She might prefer to wait until your group is more organized, though."

I wondered whether it was not so much Stephanie's reticence but really Sophie who preferred to wait for an organized youth group. We said our goodbyes and I left with some hope that a book with some answers might come soon. I was confident that it would tell me about the League. I only hoped that I'd learn about the violence from some sources somewhere. Was the killing related to the League, to the war, or something more personal? Or was it just a farm accident, as Berta suggested was likely?

11

The Friday Men's Breakfast had better attendance this week. Cal came ready for action. He seemed to assume that if I could report on a successful tour, that a study of local history would have been the whole of my activity for the week. And he wasn't too far off the mark.

Just as I was hanging my jacket on a peg near the door at the Hilltop Café, several of the guys bounded in, already in conversation. As we found our places around the table, and the last of our group for this day arrived, Cal spoke first. Without so much as a 'good morning,' Cal hit me with an inquiry blizzard, "What have you learned about the early days, Wil? Have you been finding anything out about the Nonpartisan League, or the settlers from Norway and the Odessa Germans? You need to know about that, too, if I didn't mention it before. To understand these guys you ought to learn how it was for the foreign born folks when our country went to war with Germany in '17."

"Hey! Slow down, Cal." It was Gary who stepped into the fray. "We know you have to leave earliest, but for crying out loud. Let us order our cakes and eggs here."

I was silently thankful to Gary. I needed a moment to put my responses together. So we got Sally's attention and ordered. Gary was starting to tell the weekly joke before Cal could get his answers or ask anything more. "Sven says to Ole, 'I see you got a sign out dere in yer field says boat fer sale. You don't got no boat.'"

Before he could finish Sally came back with the coffee pot and offered a joke of her own. "Hey, if you're telling jokes about my Norski people, I've got one for you. How do you tell the difference between Gary and a canoe?" After the 'tell us' pause she finished, with a wink at Gary, "You can get a canoe to tip."

By now we didn't care if Ole had a boat, but Gary had to recover his pride, so he went on. "Sven says, 'You don't got no boat. All you got out dere is dat old Fordson tractor and a broke down hay baler.' Ole says, 'Ya. Dat's right. And dey're boat fer sale.'"

"Okay, you guys," Cal said as the laughter faded, "that's not why pastor ought to learn about our ethnic backgrounds. Don't you want to find out if he's learning enough about this end-of-the-world place where God stuck him? Enough to be of some use here?"

Now he had me. That could either be too high an expectation of me, or it could be a good excuse to go ahead and focus on that history, and the personal stories that reveal it. Now that we had our coffee and our breakfast orders were in the hands of the fry cook, I tried to give Cal some answers. "Cal, you hit me with a barrage of questions. There's not a whole lot I can tell you, but there is some. I've barely scratched the surface when it comes to the history. I did take a drive around the countryside, Sage County and all. And I did find what I'm pretty certain was the farmstead I was looking for. You could see where the dugout house used to be, but there wasn't any stacked sod left there. Just some roof timbers and the leveled and squared area into the cut bank. And there was a little dam with some water in it, but not much because the stream was dry. It was kind of exciting to find it, just like she described it. Except I had a hard time imagining it as the prettiest farm ever.

"But this'll be the exciting part of that trip for you, Cal," I said. "At Sage City I talked with an old cowboy—at least from the look of him he was old. The tack and empties in the back of his beat up old pickup were as good as a yodel to say this is a working cowhand. As we were talking about what I was up to out there that day, he mentioned the name A.C. Townley. He seemed to think that's what, or who, history buffs are looking for in Sage. He spat the name out with real venom, too. Told me if that was what I was looking for I should go on down to Beach and ask there. He wouldn't tell me any more than that. So, what should I make of that, I wonder?"

"Well," said Cal, "now you're getting onto some interesting stuff. I'm kind of amazed Townley could still stir that much passion. How old did you say this guy is?"

"He didn't look a day over ninety-five, or under sixty-five so far as I could tell. He'd obviously been working outdoors for years, and when he moved he was obviously in pain." I shifted to another part of my search then, saying, "You know, I got to tell you, I went to the library the other day. Sophie is locating a book for me on interlibrary. You must know of it, Cal. Titled *Political Prairie Fire*, by Morlan. I forget the first name."

"Robert, I think," said Cal. "I know you went to the library. That's why I figured I'd get away with my plan to make you tell us what you've learned."

"How'd you know I'd been to the library?"

"Sophie told me. Well, no not really. I asked her if you'd been in digging up local history. The way she told me that she wouldn't talk about which patrons come in or what they ask for let me know you had been there. Anyway, that book will be helpful for you to read, Pastor. But isn't it in our library? I read it there when we first moved here."

"I found it in the subject index. It wasn't on the shelf. Sophie checked and found out it had been tossed five years ago. If you checked it out not so long before, I wonder why it still got tossed. Don't they keep everything that has some demand?"

"I didn't check it out. I read it there in the library."

At that point Ed cut in, "There's a reason he does that, you know. You and I, we read words and lines. Cal reads a whole page at a glance."

I nodded, "Berta reads fast like that. But she still brings the books home, the fatter the better. So, Cal, you should go ahead and check them out for a day. Except maybe the books you might not want anyone to know you read. Can't imagine that you'd care who knows, though. Right now I'm waiting for the book. I did learn that the great Senator Wheeler started in politics with the NPL. But what about this Townley character? What can you tell me?"

"It's all in the book. Oh, hell's bells," Cal was saying as he looked at his watch, pushed his chair back and stood, "I'll be late for work. Townley farmed out of Beach before he started the League, so there's some almost local stuff. It's in the book. See you Sunday, or sometime."

It was nearly time for all of us to head out to other Friday activities, so I changed the subject by attempting to get some help with my sermon preparation. The Gospel was to come from Mark chapter 7 this week. I read this to the men still with me.

> Then [Jesus] returned from the region of Tyre, and went through Sidon to the Sea of Galilee, through the region of the Decapolis. And they brought to him a man who was deaf and had an impediment in his speech; and they besought him to lay his hand upon him. And taking him aside from the multitude privately, he put his fingers into his ears, and he spat and touched his tongue. And looking up to heaven, he sighed, and said to him, "Ephphatha," that is, "Be opened." And his ears were opened, his tongue was released, and he spoke plainly. And he charged them to tell no one; but the more he charged them, the more zealously they proclaimed it. They were astonished beyond measure, saying, "He has done all things well; he even makes the deaf hear and the dumb speak."

It was a moment before anyone spoke, then Ed asked, "Can you get Jesus to come down here and stick his finger in my ear, so I can get rid of this damn hearing aid?"

That's about as deep as our Bible study would be this time. I added, "Hmm, there might just be some connections here. Maybe my travels to North Dakota and to the Manor will preach after all."

I was relieved when no one bothered to ask how. That had me considering that it's a good idea to make the observation you don't want to explain just as people are ready to be on their way. We paid for our breakfasts. The tip Gary left was little bigger than his usual and he made sure we saw it. With that we all went out to face the tasks and delights of the day.

***

That Sunday the message did preach, sort of. It became a call to open up, as the Aramaic word in the Bible text, "Ephphatha," has it. I tried to connect listening to our history along with the stories and points of view of others. I maintained that open listening is needed in order to speak clearly. And Mr. Mumble-into-Hat helped me say it.

12

On Tuesday, early for the singing again, my plan was to check in with Madge. I stepped through the front door and started toward the main room where I might find Madge in her favorite sunny corner. Not seeing her immediately, I turned in the direction of Madge's room, when something struck me on the left elbow. Nilda had been trying to get my attention from the moment I started up the outdoor ramp. I was so preoccupied with questions I had for Madge that I didn't notice her even when she followed me into the building. Now, whacking me with her cane, she got my attention. Nilda pulled me aside to tell me her troubles. And my oblivion was making her more desperate. Leaning both hands on the four-footed cane to steady herself, and without so much as a 'hello' she began, "Oh, Pastor Wilson. I was waiting for you. I wanted to talk to you ever since last week, and then there was no time on Sunday. After church you were busy-busy with people making plans for the Sunday school and getting the furnace fixed and what-not. No time for a poor old woman."

I felt the sting of her accusation, but Nilda didn't wait for a reply. She wasn't done yet. "Anyway, thank you for coming early today. You've been coming around here every now and then, asking about the old days. Oh, did I ever think that was nice when you started out. A pastor who really wants to know us. So I'm flattered alright. But then I started really remembering. And I remember how I've been hurt by so much, for so long. Why? What have I done? I didn't have anything to do with it."

"With 'it'?" I asked. "Let's sit down somewhere so we can talk." We were still standing in the entrance hall. Nilda led me to her room—the single room with its family and Democratic Party wall decoration. Once seated, I looked for ways to get clarity, and to find ways to help her deal with deep feelings coming to the surface. First I probed, saying, "It sounds like you're struggling with some tough hurts. Am I hearing guilt feelings? You said you didn't have anything to do with 'it'. Can you tell me more about that?"

"That's where it all started. At least it seems that way now, looking back over the long years. That's where it started. That's why I'm not so sure I even want to remember those times."

I hoped my frustration with these veiled hints of some event didn't show. As we had always done before, we still skirted close to something, but it was again stated without an indication what the event really was. I tried a little feedback reflection of her words, checking what I was hearing, and hoping I might prompt her to say what seemed to need saying. "You don't want to remember some particular things from long ago." For good or ill, I stumbled on, "And my interest in those times has caused you pain. I'm sure sorry about that."

"Oh, it isn't you, Pastor. Well, ...sort of....maybe. But those memories were already pulling me down. Maybe for years and I didn't know it. But, you see, one day here at the Manor, Madge introduced us to a daughter who was visiting from some other place. And when she did, she said this girl—not really a girl, she was over sixty herself, but our children are always our children, aren't they. Where was I?"

"You were telling about Madge introducing her daughter."

"Oh, ya. Anyways, Madge said this daughter was from her first marriage, to Mr. Bowdler. And I knew. It all came flooding back. Now don't you breathe a word of this to anybody, please....please." It hit me like a slap upside the head. I had been so curious that hadn't paid attention to their privacy. I had spoken too freely in my quest for corroboration.

Her voice was nearly an inaudible whisper now. "Do I have to carry the burden of it? What could I have done?" Then she spoke up more boldly. "When I was young I knew God loved me. Our home was filled with his love in us. I took Jesus into my heart that time when the preacher came to the ranch, don't you know. I always tried to keep that promise. All my life. Well, I don't think God loves me anymore. He's left me all alone and it must be my fault. Why?"

Nilda always wanted prayer, even now as she felt an absence of divine care. Our pattern was that I would begin the prayer, and then at every pause she would fill in things I forgot or might yet forget to mention. That is, except last time, when we rushed off to the singing with the same sense of guilt left hanging. And we didn't pray. It was getting close to singing time now. So, rather than give some feeble response to her huge 'why?' and her emptiness, I suggested, "Nilda, the other day we rushed off to singers and didn't have our prayer. You were asking me the same sort of thing that day. Now you wonder if God can love you. I'm pretty certain God wants you to find that enfolding love again. So, let's stop here and ask God for some help, ok?" We prayed. I can't remember the words said. I think Nilda's prayer that day was beyond any words. I remember it as one of those times like St. Paul told of, when "the Spirit intercedes for us with sighs too deep for words."

I did not intend that the prayer time should close our conversation, but Nilda seemed to be ready to leave it there. It was still a little early when we walked together to the big room. I rolled the spinet piano out from the corner, found the songbooks in the cupboard and had everything ready before others arrived. As I busied myself with setting up, my thoughts wandered to some things I'd been learning about guilt and shame, and differences between them. I suddenly realized that part of my job would be to help Nilda find her way out from shame, that guilt was not the pressing problem at all. But I still had my own need to satisfy my curiosity and learn the real history of Harstad, Kirchen County and maybe of all the prairie borderlands.

13

It wasn't until the next day, sitting at my new-to-me (and to the church) desk in the new church office we had created from what had been a storage room, that I realized that my intentions to visit Madge had been thwarted for the time being. The day before I had set out to spend a pleasant hour with our proud oldest and found instead the morass of Nilda's complicated distress. Now there were other demands on my time.

People might be starting to think I only cared about those two members of the parish with phone conversations like this accumulating: "Sorry I missed your call, I was over a Prairie Manor for a while." "Oh, is someone ill?" (they may mean 'dying' but they don't say it.) "No, just visiting."

I was pondering all this when the phone rang. I pulled my feet off the desk and answered.

"Good morning, Pastor. How about that, I caught you at your new hideout away from the kids. This is Sophie."

"Good morning to you, Sophie. What can I do for you?" I said.

"I just wanted to let you know that your book has arrived. It's a four week loan. If you really read as slowly as you claim, you better come get it."

"I can come right now. I'm on shank's mare today, so maybe by the time I get back the little heater in here will start to do some good. See you in a few minutes."

A few minutes became nearly an hour. My route took me past the post office so I figured I might as well get the mail. I soon discovered that this was the time of day when the retired guys and farmers getting into the slower post-harvest mode all gathered for the post office confab. Harstad did not have home delivery mail services, so emptying P.O. boxes became a daily social event for some. It was only after some consultations on the cooler weather, possibility of an early snow storm and other issues of the day that I completed my trek to the library.

Sophie was at the front desk giving some instructions to a young assistant as I approached. She looked up and was handing me the book by the time we greeted each other. I was still digging in my wallet for a library card when Sophie stopped me, letting me know that she had the information she needed. Then she turned back to her assistant, a strikingly pretty young woman with unnaturally black hair who stood a head taller than Sophie. I couldn't recall having seen her before, and I would remember. She was that good looking.

They seemed to be all business so no introductions were made. Rather than hurry back to my under-heated office I found a comfortable chair among the current newspapers and magazines and began to check the table of contents and read the preface to *Political Prairie Fire: The Nonpartisan League, 1915-1922* on loan from the Montana Historical Society Library. The copyright page said 1955. This was the most recent work on the subject that we could find. Did it completely die in 1922 then? The answer to my thought question could only be, "Read the damn book."

My reading was briefly interrupted a couple times. It seemed the wives visited the library while their husbands argued politics and weather at the post office. After fifteen or twenty minutes of reading and greeting, Sophie came over and said, "Karen's got things in hand here and I'm ready for a break. Can I buy you a cup of coffee?"

'Buying' a cup of coffee turned out to be mugs of instant coffee in the library's work room—a former teacher's lounge and prep area at the back of the old school building. Something was on Sophie's mind. I assumed I knew what it was and got the first word in our conversation. "We got off to a good start on a youth group Sunday night. The kids went out and recruited advisors. They convinced that new teacher couple that came to town a few weeks ago to help them. I sure hope we can get Stephanie to come and join."

Sophie was giving me a blank look until I mentioned her daughter. "Oh. We entirely forgot about the meeting. But Steph is kind of shy, you know. Maybe it's just as well to go slow. Who did you say were your advisors?"

"A young couple, Kevin and Julia Lahti. They're both first year teachers. He teaches the business classes and some P.E. at the high school. Julia teaches third grade at Jefferson. I do hope Steph will come. Sunday after next we'll meet again. I think there's something to be said for giving it a try soon, while we're all newcomers at it."

"Okay, we'll try. But Pastor, that wasn't the reason I wanted to talk to you. It's about your historical research. It has me curious, too. I've been having some fun trying to get some of our old-timer patrons to tell me what they might know about the events and situations you've been asking about."

"Really. Do they skirt all around the real issues and almost but never quite say it—like my Prairie Manor friends?"

"Well, yes. There is some of that. And some people refuse to tell me anything at all. And that just amazes me. My experience of the older folks everywhere I've worked has been that you just flip the switch, they turn on and tell all kinds of stories. Even if it's the same story told over and over at the same sitting. And the folks here do that alright, but certain subjects that I ask about seem to switch them off again."

"What subjects seem to stop the story telling?"

"If I bring up the Nonpartisan League the typical response is that they've all left. That's if they admit to knowing about it at all. 'They're not here anymore,' they say. And that seems to be the end of it. Gone, so it doesn't matter any longer. If I bring up the First World War, I might hear about the family members who served in the military but they won't talk about what it was like here at home. So, I haven't really learned anything first hand. That's why I wanted to kind of alert you. I hope you're not opening a can of worms here. I'm just as curious about the local history, but I worry if you push too hard, it might make it difficult to stay as our pastor here. And from what else I hear on the grapevine, we don't want to lose you anytime soon, you see."

"Well, I'm flattered that I have support. And I'm pretty cautious by nature. So I'm more worried that your worry will get to me. I think we're very close to hearing the whole story from the ladies at the Manor. So, maybe if I just avoid being too public about what I'm asking about. Will that put us all at ease, do you think?"

"I hope so. Better drink up. Instant coffee gets even worse lukewarm. And I need to get back to my job, too. Unless I miss my guess, when you get back to the office it'll either be too warm or someone will have been there, found heat on in an empty office and shut if off for you and it'll be cold again."

"It's good talking with you. I think our history is still defining our community in more ways than we can acknowledge. And that's why it's so important to understand it. Take care, Sophie."

"You too. Take care, Reverend Wil. Enjoy your reading."

As I headed back to the office to get started I was thinking that I probably would enjoy it.

***

I was beginning to get used to the fact that country parsons can sometimes go days without a phone call or visit that they don't initiate themselves. Apparently this isn't the case when we most want the alone time. I found the office toasty warm by the time I returned, so I turned the heater off, put my feet up, opened the book and started again at the preface:

> Rocketing to prominence in the early days of World War I, the Nonpartisan League in North Dakota and adjoining states achieved a measure of political success well beyond that which has been the lot of most movements of protest in the history of the United States. Not only was it to control for some years the government of one state, elect state officials and legislators in a number of midwestern and western states, and send several of its representatives to the Congress—its impact was to help shape the destinies of a dozen states and the political philosophies of an important segment of the nation's voters.[*]

At that moment the phone rang. As I was answering it the office door opened and my day changed direction. I had to remind myself that interruptions were an important part of my job. It looked like Political Prairie Fire would become bedtime reading. It did, but I found other time over the next couple weeks to read to the end.

At our first long visit Madge had said, "I've seen wet and I've seen dry." Now I could visit her with some information from other sources, mostly from the first half of the book, that might encourage her to tell the story of the 'dry' she had experienced.

---

[*]Robert L. Morlan, Political Prairie Fire: The Nonpartisan League, 1915-1922. (Minneapolis, University of Minnesota Press, 1955). Preface.

14

A Tuesday afternoon pattern was developing. After welcoming our afternoon kindergartener home and admiring her papers and projects, I would head for Prairie Manor to visit around, especially with my two storytellers, before our little entertainment time. This week I would be sure to visit with Madge. I even began to rehearse the conversation as I walked the mile from home to the Manor.

But I neglected to consider one consequence as my routine became so regular. My pattern was observed. It also established a pattern for someone else. Nilda met me just inside the front door with her cane ready to strike if I should try to slip past her. "Hello, Pastor. I see you came over early again. It's so nice of you."

"Good afternoon, Mrs. Ruud. How are you feeling today?"

"Oh, Pastor Wilson, you don't have to be so formal. Call me Nilda, please. And I am feeling pretty well, thank you. I've been thinking and I've been praying. I've been remembering our talk last week. Now I'm coming to believe it'll help if I tell you all about Papa and Walt."

Hearing this had me thinking—and, I suppose, praying, 'How can I get out of doing this today? I really want the time with the other one now. Can honesty possibly help?' So, to Nilda I said, "I'm really glad that you're feeling better about things, and your prayers are letting God help you get there. Today, though, I think I need to spend some time with other folks here, including Madge, of course. Especially Madge. I haven't had a chance to visit with her for a couple weeks, you see. And, it occurs to me that it would probably be better for us to talk about these things when our time isn't cut off by the singing time. How about I come over in a day or two and we'll take the time we need then?"

Well, by the time I'd plowed through that whole field, what could she say but, "Well, that's fine then, Pastor. But don't you forget. You come tomorrow afternoon, at this time, and I'll be ready."

Her bright mood deflated, she tromped off toward her room waving her cane in front of her as if to clear a path. I just shook my head thinking, 'Whatever I do, it's wrong.'

***

I sought out Madge then, and found her in her favorite spot in the big room just as I expected I would. "Hello, Mrs. Carter. It's Pastor Wil. How are you today?"

"You think I didn't know who you are? Come, sit down."

I sat, running through the questions in my head, about her first husband Elwin, about the killing, and about the League. I had my questions ready, but Madge would remind me soon enough that she controls our agenda.

"Why so formal, Pastor? My name is Madge."

It was foolish to think I needed to, but I explained anyway. "I read something the other day that the generations older than mine prefer titles of respect; that too much first naming makes it seem like we don't matter, or deserve respect. But Nilda Ruud, reacted just like you did."

"Pshaw. Whoever wrote that advice has never been to Montana."

And yet, she always referred to her late husband as Mr. Carter. I leaned forward a little, ready to ask about Elwin, the husband she called by first name, but Madge started first. And it was as if she had stayed there in her farm house memory for the two weeks since we last talked.

"I had two tin boxes on the kitchen shelf. That kitchen felt so roomy, with a table where we could all sit down to dinner, and a wash stand that was just for washing. We built that house almost on top of the well, so the hand pump was right there on the porch behind the kitchen. I could get my wash water, heat it on the stove—we moved the little cook stove over from the soddy and it was still our only heat. Anyway, I had water right outside the door. Didn't even have to go out in the rain or snow to pump a bucketful. I had shelves for the crockery and my pots and pans. I had a little pantry and we dug out a cellar for spuds and all, and for storms, too. Wait. That's not what I set out to tell you. Where was I?"

"Was it about the tin boxes – one for seeds and for money to buy seed?

"Oh, the boxes, that's right. I was wanting to tell you about when Elwin got started in the League. Are you writing this down? You should, I truly believe. This here is oral history we're doing, don't you know. I wasn't thinking of our talks like that, but there was a young college girl with one of those tape recorder machines here one day getting Ferguson to telling his story. I didn't want to talk to her though. I was saving it to tell you. Are you writing this down? You should."

"No Madge. I didn't bring paper with me. But I do write notes in my journal when I get home. I'll bring a notebook with me next time. I didn't think you'd like having me writing while we talk."

"Maybe I won't. Elwin would've had it wrote down for you before he even told it. Longest thing I ever wrote was a grocery list or an order for the yard goods wholesaler. But Elwin would write out his plans, how he would close the sale. I mean he'd write it down, what he would say to the other farmers to get them into the League. That was later, of course. I still didn't tell you, did I."

"Tell me what?"

"About when the organizer came to tell Elwin about the Nonpartisan League and get him to join up, of course. So I'm telling you now. I had those tin boxes, and I'd been saving up pretty good from selling my eggs and produce and such to the town folks and rails."

"What are 'rails'?" I asked.

"Why, the railroad workers, of course. Didn't you know that? Some of those families didn't even keep a garden. Guess they didn't see the point if they got told to move, which they did often enough. They led me to the best customer. I was making some money at it because the dining car cooks knew my eggs would be fresh and candled proper, so they knew they got good value. I'd send Elwin with five dozen eggs that he'd put on the spur line at Sage to take to the main road down to Beach."

Her answer was new information, so I didn't bother to remind her that she had already told me quite a bit about the NPL visit. I let her say it again in hopes that she would be able to tell the whole story this time. She went through it very much the same as before, about 'big biz' and the Ford car, and was able to get to more of the account.

"The organizer had Elwin convinced. Even though he didn't want to be labeled a socialist, the ideas about helping the farmers get control away from the big boys in Minnesota had him ready to join. I still wasn't sure it was really real, but we were farmers together so I figured we better take a chance. I did feel a need to support my man. The organizer man told all about the League's newspaper that we'd get and that we could pay the $16 annual membership with a post-dated check to be cashed after harvest. That's when I thought of my tin box. I got up from the table, making like that was just going to pour them some more coffee. I took the pot from the stove, filled their cups, and then pulled the box from the high shelf. I took it over to the wash stand where I could count with my back to the men. I counted those coins, then counted again. There was eight silver dollars in there. All told, I had seventeen dollars and thirty-two cents. And don't ask me why I can remember it so exact. I don't know why. What I know is I had more than enough for seeds. That's certain. But not enough for both seeds and League. I always had big dreams for my garden, you see. And it really wasn't about seeds, don't you know. My boys needed new boots. I did it anyway, though. Instead of after harvest, I told Elwin he should write that check for next week, and I would deposit my egg money. I still didn't trust enough to give the man my cash, don't you know."

"I can understand that," I said. "I suspect that kind of caution has served you well other times, too."

She nodded assent to that, and said, "That's been my way: slow to give trust, but then slower still to take it away once I give it. And now I'm the oldest, you know."

I said, "I've been reading about the NPL. It sounds like it must have been an exciting time of big changes in North Dakota. There's a quote in the book that sounds a lot like what you've been telling me about. And since you started to tell it last time, I even wrote down that quote." I reached in my shirt pocket, unfolded the paper and was about to read. "Well, looks like I have some paper with me after all, and the whole back side I could've used to take notes. Oh well. Listen to what it says from the organizer's correspondence course:

By way of a clincher for the "almost persuaded" the following was suggested:

"Here's the thing in a nutshell." Here he pulls a handful of change out of his pocket, two quarters, three dimes, three nickels, and five pennies—just a dollar in change.

"Now here is a dollar. For every dollar's worth of stuff you raise on this farm you get just 46 cents." Here he counts out and lays in one pile one quarter, two dimes, and a penny.

"This is what you get. But here," laying in another pile the other quarter, dime, three nickels, and four pennies— "here is what the other fellow gets—the fellow who didn't put in a day plowing and planting and harvesting. Now what you want is more of this pile. You want your share of that dollar the consumer pays for what you raise by back-breaking work. The other fellow gobbles this because he is organized. He controls the market—he makes the laws—he gets the money. Do you want more of this pile of money which belongs to you, Mr. Blank?"

Now he has the farmer where he has to answer "yes." He can't say he doesn't want that money for he does—any man does. And yet that "yes" carries with it the organization, too. It is rather a hard thing for a farmer to refuse to join after that "yes" . . . Any method which makes it harder for him to turn you down than to say yes and join, is a good method. Work out the one that fits your way of managing the solicitation.*

"Does that sound at all familiar, Madge?"

"Oh, my yes. And that's what Elwin wanted to do, too, once he started reading that Nonpartisan Leader magazine. He never got hired to organize, but organize he did. And paid for it." Madge paused, wiped her nose, and took a couple deep breaths before she continued.

"And paid for it," she repeated. "Elwin was so different from Mr. Carter. God rest the both of 'em. Elwin brought us west to be independent farmers. And soon enough he was burning with that fever to bring all the farmers together. We were finding out that if we were going to be independent of the mills and railroads the farmers had to be dependent on each other." Madge paused then, as if to let the statement sink in. Then she added, "My, my, but if I ain't turning philosophical in my dotage."

"And with a valuable insight too, I have to say."

"They were very different men, my hubbies, but two sides of the same coin in a way. Mr. Carter was natural born for business. He'd look around for what people seemed to need or want, whatever was missing from the market, and he'd try to fill that need. And was that ever a challenge in the thirties, let me tell you. Did I tell you about how we kept store in those days? Seems like I told somebody lately. Was that you?"

---

* Op. cit. Morlan. p. 30.

"Yes, that was me. You gave me a fascinating account of how you and Charles, Mr. Carter, rose to those challenges and made a good life even in the hardships."

"Strange, isn't it Pastor? I had all those years with Mr. Carter, and he was so good to my children and then our children, too, his and mine. But it's strange. I sit here a decrepit old lady with nothing to do but remember, and it is those few years with Elwin that always stand out. Must be something about young love, do you think so, Pastor Wil?"

"Tell me about Elwin, then. He got involved with the Nonpartisan League. I think I'm hearing you say that was really important. What made it end so soon? Did he put his life on the line for the League?"

"Oh, now you're touching on it, Mister, but do I have to remember everything?"

"I don't know. I'm getting a feeling that maybe, yes, maybe you need to. And I really hope that feeling is for your need, not just because I'm so interested to hear about it all." I hadn't meant to confess the self-doubt, the doubt that had entered my middle of the night prayers. It just came out before I could stop it. Madge either didn't hear that or didn't care. It was clear that she was remembering something, but she could not bring herself to share it, at least not yet.

She continued her story, avoiding whatever she wasn't prepared to remember. "I was thinking about how Elwin and Mr. Carter were so different in some ways and the same in others. I did find me two men worth marrying, you see. But Elwin, when he started reading that Leader paper with the cartoons about evil Big Biz, and he got the bug for organizing, he saw the big companies as the tyrant we had to overthrow. But Mr. Carter, with that little store, he saw those fat rich men as the big challenge. He'd dream and scheme about how he could get rich like that. He was all business when it came to the store. He wanted to be Sears AND Roebuck. I didn't like to discourage him but I couldn't keep quiet, don't you know. I just wanted that little store to succeed and take care of the customers better than anybody else on the street. Mr. Carter dreamed of having lots of stores while I dreamed of having happy customers of the whole town. My joy was seeing the girls in the pretty dresses their mamas had sewed well from the gingham I helped them pick out, and I'd taught them tips for nice seams and a good fit."

"So Mr. Carter kind of envied the rich corporation owners, but Elwin saw it as a conflict, the other side to fight against?" I said this trying hard not to take sides. I managed to avoid the word 'enemy' but not 'envy'. At least I didn't say Mr. Carter 'coveted'. I really wanted Madge to get back to talk about Elwin, and that conflict. The way she would home in on the subject, then go off on another tangent was beginning to frustrate me. I had to remind myself that my purpose was that she tell a story she needed to tell, not necessarily the one I wanted to hear.

"You're right about that, Pastor Tim, er-um Pastor Wil. Elwin took to the good fight. And, in spite of everything I'm still proud of him. He wanted so bad to be hired as an organizer. He was ready to buy that correspondence course like what you read off your paper there. But the debts was piling up, and he always put me and the kiddies first. And we did need him home on the farm if we were going to make it. Always looking ahead for one more good harvest. Then, after that, maybe. But he organized anyway. He did even ride with the man who brought us into the League a couple times. Funny I can't remember his name when I can remember seventeen dollars and thirty-two cents. My boy Ralph must get it from me—he's a certified public accountant up in Great Falls. ....Where was I?"

"You have reason to be real proud of your sons and daughters, Madge," I said. "You were telling about Elwin organizing."

"Oh, Elwin would talk up the League with the other farmers when he went to town for a market day in Sage City. Some of the other farmers from over that way would recall when Mr. Townley had his big flax growing project over to Beach. And some of them said they just couldn't trust him. Even though he only failed because he counted on good rains at the right time, just like the rest of us. And a blizzard at the wrong time can be the end before you build any equity. But, still. He was a big idea man, and some just can't trust that. Jealous, I'd say. See, Elwin had organized me into a true believer by that time."

Just then Rachel came bustling in with her arms filled with sheet music, song books and even a hymnal. She plopped it all on the spinet piano and made a show of the effort to move the instrument out where she could sit at the keyboard. I tried to avoid looking that way, pretending not to notice that she was there. I didn't want to end the conversation with Madge so abruptly.

Madge noticed her too, though, saying, "I think that woman wants you to help, Pastor." By then the task was done. Rachel started playing to get our attention, and others of the group began drifting in. I started to get up and wish Madge well.

As I was reaching down to her for a light hug she shared parting words, "Elwin kept promoting, you see. It was when he tried organizing over here in Montana—that's what I guess I have to tell you about. So you ask about that. I'll tell it. It's just hard to think about, don't you know. It hurts. But hey, I'm the oldest. And that's a good thing to be."

The thought took hold of me as I turned to the next thing, 'it's hard and it hurts.' So it wasn't particularly easy to get up and make the shift from those parting words to singing old tin pan alley songs with our group. We weren't really much of a choir, anyway. It got harder when Rachel told us to turn in our mimeographed and stapled songbooks to page 8. I waved and shook my head, trying to veto that plan, but no one seemed to notice. So, the group launched into "Smiles" and the tears streamed down Madge's face. But she was grinning the whole time. I guess the others were right to ignore my frantic gestures.

15

The next day I left the house promptly at 3:15 for the walk to Prairie Manor with one stop along the way to empty our box at the post office. Nilda had quite deftly converted my vague offer to stop by in a day or two into a specific promise to keep a scheduled 3:30 appointment.

Nilda did not meet me at the door with the four-footed wicked whacker this time. I found her at her room dozing in the deep chair. If she hadn't been expecting me I'd have quietly attempted to leave a calling card on the nightstand and tiptoe away. It wouldn't have worked, of course. Two steps into the room and she was awake—before I tapped on the open door or said anything.

"Well, hello there, Pastor! I'll have to tell everyone. Pastor Wil keeps his promises."

"Hi, Nilda. Please don't say that. People will expect me to live up to a higher standard, and I'll lose the good reputation soon enough."

"Pastor Wil, I want to show you something my daughter found and brought over. Get that shoebox, if you will. It's right over there on the shelf under the nightstand."

I retrieved the box. Its loose torn lid slipped as I tried to hold it with one hand, nearly scattering the many old pictures it contained. With both thumbs holding the lid in place, I delivered the box to Nilda and sat down in the chair that always faced the window looking out on the park across the street. She held the box on her lap, pushed the lid aside, and passed an old photograph over to me. A young man and woman, young enough looking that you might say boy and girl, he in a tight fitting three button suit and vest, she in a lacy white gown and holding a small bouquet of flowers—spring wild flowers, perhaps?—looked out from the picture with the stiff expressions that mark the need to hold the pose through the ancient film's slow exposure time.

Without comment Nilda passed another stiff old photo, torn and taped across a corner, of the same young man in a military uniform with corporal stripes on the sleeves. Then she handed the whole box to me, saying, "Go ahead. Look through those if you want."

I flipped through the scattered pile of old pictures for a minute or two. Then without getting up I set the box on the foot of her neatly-made bed, keeping back the two she'd especially chosen. "Was this taken on your wedding day?"

"Nearly, Pastor, nearly. Only the rich town folks could bring a photographer to a wedding in those days, at least out here. Walt and I stood up in front of the house, with family and neighbors around. We said our vows with the German Congregational preacher when he came over from Dakota somewhere. Oh, it all comes back to me now. What a day. That stiff preacher. What was his name? Oh, well, doesn't matter, does it? He was such a shy man, you wondered, 'how could he possibly spread any Gospel if he's afraid to talk to people?' Then he'd slip into his preaching manner, and everything changed. He'd have everybody ready to confess sins they hadn't even thought of yet and turn to Jesus right now. Most would repent and forget, but not me. I took Jesus into my heart that very day, my wedding day. I never looked back. Walt and I became one before God, and I found God in the middle of everything. That preacher thought he was there to organize more prayer meetings and ended up in a wedding. I believe we rubbed some of the shyness out of that awkward man that day, too."

"What an amazing wedding story. Thank you for sharing it. What a blessing!"

"I had that special dress, there in the picture, all ready for the wedding, almost since Christmas. That's when Walt proposed, you see. Walt said we'd go to town and get the preacher to marry us there, but it was winter. When the thaw came, so did the spring calving and planting. He was already working as a hand for Papa, since before we got engaged. So when the reverend came to the ranch at branding, that was the right time. That was April 2, 1917. Four days later we were at war—America, not me and Walt. The picture was later. We took the train to Miles City, that was our honeymoon, when President Wilson—are you related?—when he signed the conscription law. I put on my dress and we went to a picture studio. We laughed about how odd the picture would be with me in a fancy white dress and Walt in his almost worn out wool trousers and braces . And we didn't even think that was odd at the actual wedding. The picture man put him in that coat and vest, and put him behind so you can't see the knee patches, can you. Then Walt went down to the army war office and joined up. He decided not to wait and be drafted. It's like he had to prove he was the most patriotic, being German and all. Oh, did it ever hurt when the day came a few weeks later, to see him go off and leave us to farm without him. We'd just got started fixing up the homestead cabin and living there. When Walt left I moved back into the house with Mom and Papa to wait for the birth—Magda was on the way.

"That other picture I showed you. Where is it? Oh, you've still got it. Good. Walter sent me that picture after they made him a corporal. He was a strong farmer, like so many, but they soon found out he was smart, too. And the others at the training camp in Kansas looked up to him right away. So, they made him a corporal. And took his picture in his uniform with the stripe on his sleeve. You see that?" she said pointing to the details in the picture. "So we had some pride. I could hide how scared I was behind the pride I had in my good soldier man. I'm so happy Magda found those pictures."

"Me, too," I replied. "So, having a German name was a problem here? But not at the army camp in Kansas?"

There was a long pause before Nilda responded. When she did, it was in answer only to my second question, saying, "The US Army was looking for any man who could lead at that time. Walt came home a sergeant, but that isn't all." We waited through another long pause.

I finally repeated back to Nilda, "That isn't all?"

"Life can change so quick, can't it. In the blink of an eye everything is different. On my wedding day I still thought the war in Europe was something we sent relief goods for. At the end of the same week we were in the war, America was. Barely say 'I do' and my husband is getting ideas of joining up."

"Uh-huh. Something we send relief." And I began to sing a little ditty, "All the folks at our house are busy as can be, sewing for the Bel-gee-ans that live across the sea."

Nilda nearly jumped out of her chair. "Where did you learn that? That was on one of the silly records we used to play on our neighbor's, the Lintner's, Victrola after Christian Endeavor meetings. Really, where did you hear that."

"Just like you. My grandparents in Wisconsin had an old Victrola that we brought down from the attic once when we were visiting. My dad and uncle found the old Uncle Josh record and the song stuck in my head, for some reason."

"Well, that does bring back memories."

We sat in silence then for longer than just a pause. Finally Nilda said, "I'm so glad you came today, Pastor Wil. This has been a nice visit."

We had our traditional prayer time. I started as usual, and Nilda added many mumbled phrases until she stopped me with a more vocal "Amen." As I replayed our conversation in my thoughts during the walk home I realized that this had not been the visit I had expected. I thought it had probably not gone quite as Nilda intended the previous day when she insisted that we meet right away, either. Her fairly abrupt end left me very aware that the conversation had really not ended.

There was much more that she would soon be ready, even anxious, to tell. Subjects she could only approach, but not bring into the open just yet.

16

On Friday morning that same week our regular Men's Lectionary Breakfast table at the Hilltop Café was already filling up when I arrived, and I was five minutes early. I had to wonder as I set my books on a corner of the table, 'What are we doing right, that our little sessions are becoming popular?'

Before I could get seated, Cal introduced me to a friend he had brought with him. He told me that Joseph Schmidt was another local history buff. Cal said, "I've been telling Joe about your interest in the early settler days around here, and the Nonpartisan League and such. So I convinced him to tag along this morning."

"Well, it's good to meet you, Joe. Is the NPL something you've studied some, too?" I asked.

Joe took a deep breath and began the lecture, while others at the table gave signals that they'd occupy their time with side conversations. "You know, Reverend Wilson, the League does come into it some, but I've been riding around this territory for forty years now, and I believe there's something much bigger than political clubs and fences. I'm convinced that the land has its own story, too, and we ought to pay attention to it."

Just then our last three regulars arrived. Those already present jumped up to help pull a small table over to adjoin the big one. They made as much commotion as they could connecting the tables and arranging the larger setting. I was beginning to get the hint. I was intrigued by Joe's perspective and wanted to let him go on. At the same time I couldn't help but be amused that a church group, supposedly a Bible study, could show such discomfort when someone seems to be leading toward something spiritual.

Cal was probably not trying to give me an out when he said, "Pastors come and go around here, but Wil is a rare one who actually seems interested in the history here. Pastor Tim would just get us to agree with his interpretation of the Bible, say a prayer and we'd eat our breakfast." He was more likely encouraging Joe to continue and the others to be attentive.

I took it as a way out, saying, "You're probably being a little hard on Pastor Tim, Cal. Maybe he had some of that right. Our breakfast is supposed be about the Bible readings that I'll be preaching on. Maybe we should start with our study, and then let's get spiritual—that was about to happen, I think—then let's get spiritual about the history of the land. I, for one, am really intrigued by what you started to say, Joe."

Sally, our amazing waitress and part owner of the Hilltop Café, had been busying herself at the counter, allowing our discussion to go on without interruption. We were her first and only diners so far that morning. She took advantage of the opening now, bringing menus and coffee. Menus were just a formality. We were all ready to order by the time the coffee mugs were filled. Once Sally had gone we would begin again.

"Looks like Gary won't be with us today. Can we have our meeting without his weekly joke? Or does somebody have one?" I asked.

Ed responded in fits and starts, "There's the one....oh, never mind. I can't remember the punch line."

I took a sip of tongue-scalding coffee and said, "So let's start with the Gospel lesson for Sunday." With a side glance at Cal, I went on, "Maybe I'll find out my interpretation needs some help from you guys. The lesson I want to focus on is Mark 9:30-37." Then I read from my Revised Standard Version Bible:

They went on from there and passed through Galilee. He would not have anyone know it; for he was teaching his disciples, saying to them, "The Son of man will be delivered into the hands of men, and they will kill him; and when he is killed, after three days he will rise." But they did not understand the saying, and they were afraid to ask him.

And they came to Capernaum; and when he was in the house he asked them, "What were you discussing on the way?" But they were silent; for on the way they had discussed with one another who was the greatest. And he sat down and called the twelve; and he said to them, "If any one would be first, he must be last of all and servant of all." And he took a child, and put him in the midst of them; and taking him in his arms, he said to them; "Whoever receives one such child in my name receives me; and whoever receives me, receives not me but him who sent me."

The pause for throat clearing and spoon rattling after I set the book aside was shorter than usual this day. Joseph asked, "From where? You read, 'They went on from there.' Where is 'there'?"

I had to find the reference. "Well, let's see. At the beginning of chapter nine Jesus takes Peter, James and John up a mountain. It's a pivotal scene that's called the Transfiguration. And they come down to where the other disciples and lots of people seem to be. Jesus heals a boy. So, that doesn't quite answer where, in relation to Capernaum, does it. Ah, but wait. Back up a little more. They had been traveling through Caesarea Philippi. Does that help any?" I turned to the map section in the back of my Bible to show where Caesarea Philippi is in relation to the Sea of Galilee and the town of Capernaum.

Joseph said, "Thank you. I don't know why, but I do love maps. But I'm not much for studying the Bible. Is it a confession to admit that here? I haven't read the Bible much at all since I escaped from Sunday school. No doubt you want to preach about that first and last, servant of all stuff, or Jesus telling them how he'll die and all."

I nodded assent, "Well, yeah. Those seem like the points that stand out."

"But Reverend," Joseph said, "what I notice in your reading is the movement—how they're always going someplace, going somewhere else. While you read it I was thinking to myself, 'Is that just in Mark, or is that the way all the Gospels tell it?' Anyway, what it says to me is that the land, the place, is important. We come here to Harstad, or our recent ancestors do, from all kinds of places and the land changes us, we become people of this land in unpredictable ways. And it sounds to me like maybe Jesus understood that, too. Like he took his followers into certain places for certain things. Like up on that mountain for Transfiguration. And Caesarea Philippi—that's away from his home country, right? I'm seeing this connection here, when you guys do your Bible stuff and so on. I'm seeing this connection that maybe it can help you see where you really are, after all. Is anybody with me on that?"

The slow nodding of heads, and even slower non-committal vocal responses indicated that Joseph had raised some questions for us, but we weren't sure what they mean to us.

Sally brought breakfasts and re-filled our coffee, so Cal took this opportunity to change the subject. As the others dug into their eggs, he asked, "Have you talked with your lady friends at the Manor this week, Wil?"

"Boy howdy, am I ever hearing some oral history," I replied. "I heard some about A.C. Townley and the NPL, and some of the attitude that came from knowing him as a big flax farmer out of Beach. I heard how some didn't trust him because of that. And I thought I might hear about it from the other point of view. That visit ended up with stories that hinted about the way World War I interrupted their lives." I said all this with enthusiasm until a thought flew into my head that cut me short. The question had focused on the ladies I visited. How was it that I had so casually let so much private conversation become public? How quickly small town ways had overcome everything I'd learned at seminary about keeping trust and confidences.

The guys fidgeted, but no one spoke during my odd pause. I tried for a biblical connection then and continued. "So, you talk about how the land shapes us. And Jesus did let the locations help teach his lessons about love and hope, I believe. We are still doing Bible study, right? Anyway, I hear things from folks and from some of you about land and weather and the old days; about events on the other side of the ocean having their effect on who the people here would become. And I'm having a hard time keeping up with my other responsibilities when I just want to sit around swapping stories."

Those who hadn't been doing much talking had mostly finished their pancakes and eggs. Cal turned around in his chair to look at the wall clock, saw the time and jumped up, saying, "Whoa! I'm pushing the time again. Can I drop you at your house, Joe?"

"No, Cal. Pastor Wilson can get me home," Joseph answered. He looked to me for affirmation, so I nodded in reply, "No problem. You get on to your water trucking."

"Okay," Cal said, "You should know that riding across town in Wil's Renault is an adventure. I hope you're ready."

With that, Cal grabbed his jacket from its peg beside the door and headed out. Joe and I accepted another coffee refill. When Ed turned down the offer, the other men also refused more coffee. As they emptied their mugs, each of them excused themselves and left us. I knew, because I'd been told, that my predecessor Pastor Tim would have made them all stay through a long-winded prayer. Somehow, knowing that fact did not make me feel guilty about its omission on this day.

Joe had some ideas to test out with me and I was ready to get started. And, he had already promoted me from 'reverend' to 'pastor'. That felt good, too.

***

I had an idea to test with Joe, too, so I started the dialogue. "You know, Joe, our little group didn't seem to add much to the thoughts you were sharing. And Cal really wanted to get into the local history angle. I think he was kind of disappointed in me for insisting on the Bible study today. Sometimes we hardly get to any of that. In fact, sometimes instead of Bible Study our talk is something else with the same initials." Coffee spurted out Joe's nose when he caught what I had just said. "Today I really needed a spark to get my preparations for Sunday started. By the way, your observations about the land really help. It approaches the message from an angle I hadn't ever noticed. What I was just thinking, though, is this: Maybe we need to start another group to study local history. If we could pull that together I think Sophie Kettle, the librarian, might be interested. What do you think? We could meet at a time when Cal doesn't have to rush off to his job in the oil patch."

"I don't know, Wilford. Can I first name you?"

"I've been calling you Joe without your permission. Just Wil is good."

"Okay, Wil it is. So Wil, here's the deal. I have too many meetings to go to already. That's not what I expected retirement to be, but I enjoy myself. I promised myself I wouldn't add any new obligation without subtracting something else. But I can't bring myself to quit anything. So we'll see. I'll have to think about it. But for right now, do you have a little time this morning?"

I really needed to get at the sermon and other preparations for Sunday in order to keep my regular Saturday off with my family, but this conversation sounded more interesting, so I answered, "I have some time. There are some things I'll need to get at, but they can wait a little while."

"Well, good. When you have to go, just say so. Would it be okay with you if we take our coffee over to a booth on the smokers' side of the room?"

On the way, I stopped at the coat hooks and grabbed the pipe from my jacket. I was trying to quit, but still carried one with me. And it would let Joe be more comfortable feeding his habit. We moved to the ashtray side and Joe had the first of several cigarettes burning by the time we sat down. I packed and lit my pipe, which promptly went out. I didn't bother to relight since it was really just something to do with my hands, anyway.

"So, you want to join the Nonpartisan League, do you?" Joe asked.

Joe's question startled me. For a moment I took him seriously. "Are you an organizer for the NPL?"

Joe laughed, "No, the League is long gone from Montana. It never was very big here, except in the northeast corner where if fed into the Communist Party. Burton K. Wheeler used it for his political career, but that was about its only hour of real fame in Montana. Over in North Dakota, now, there it's still important—always just under the surface. They combined with the Democrats over there in the '50's, but they didn't disappear."

"I read that in the book I've been reading about it," I said. "Interesting how the parties shift. It mostly used the Republican party in the years I've been reading and hearing about."

"You named that right. They used all political parties for their purposes. Never really non-partisan, they were more trans-partisan, I'd say. Primary elections were a new thing, and they worked the system well to advance their men. But you see, here's the deal. The League was about where the power finds its center. They set out to take the power that was all in the corporate board rooms of the Twin Cities, and put it with the farmers—by way of the Nonpartisan League's organizing sway. A grass-roots organization, with A.C. Townley always in charge. It did a lot of good, don't get me wrong. But, where is the power really? I believe that when all is said and done, the power is still in the soil, not the farmers who till it or the merchants who sell it six ways from Sunday. It is the land and the climate that determines more about us than we ever want to admit."

"So, it's the land and location that stands out first for you," I said, "like in our Bible reading earlier, then. What stands out for me, on a Friday, is to wonder: Will it preach? My vision gets a real short range about this time in the week."

"You ask will it preach," Joe replied. "Well, that depends on what you're really selling, doesn't it. What do you want the folks to buy?"

With a chuckle I replied, "Reduce my high calling to selling breakfast cereal, will you. I want them, and you too, to have life, but life with the eternal in it here and now."

"Let Mikey try it," Joe said, and then went back to his preaching to a one person congregation. "People have tried to settle on this prairie for hundreds, maybe thousands, of years. Except in a few spots along the big Missouri, they have always been, or ended up, nomads. Now we build fences and towns, drill wells, push the plains people onto reservations, and think we can go on like this forever. I'm telling you, the land will have its way. We'll either learn to follow the game, like the people before us, or we'll just dry up and blow away. This land cannot support what we're doing to it….and under it. I just hope we leave enough life in the land for the Crow and Lakota and Cheyenne when they take it back."

The preaching was becoming a wee bit polemical. I had no idea how, or whether, to respond. Joe seemed to interpret my body language as a real discomfort with his ideas. He may even have been right. He didn't let it stop him, but he shifted his lecture to his own family's connection to the land.

"I come from German stock, German-American by now. The name Joseph Schmidt probably gives you a clue. My ancestors came to America from Russia. Germans who became wheat farmers in Russia, in Ukraine, near the Black Sea. They moved there by invitation, and to escape Prussian army conscription. Then, another Tsar, who asserted power in a different way, couldn't abide the immigrants, and pushed us out. Eventually some of us ended up here. Your church is full of us, you know. Watch out for those German pietists there. If someone comes into your office shouting at you in German, you'd better know that you've been utterly cursed.

"Anyway, here's the deal," Joe continued, "think about all those movements over the decades. We always seem to think we're settlers, but in the long run we're nomads, too. So, why is it that I get such rude treatment in my family when I say it? Why should we expect a future so at odds with our history? And why should we think we have more right to the place just because the powerful invite us? What makes us have more right to it than the ones with even less power who were cast aside? That's in both Ukraine and Montana, by the way."

"Well, you said your ancestors always claimed to be permanent settlers wherever they were," I said. "So, there's that history, too. No one likes the prophet, because true prophecy always seems to mean hardship ahead. Always a wilderness on the way before we can find the promised land. But we want to think we're already living in the promised land, somehow promised just to us, so we don't want to hear different. And it is a pretty good place, so how can we be sure we aren't?" I was thinking out loud. "Before we go, and that needs to be very soon, let me pull you back to the settling in this area, back around the turn of the century and after. People came out here with promises of bounty from the railroads' homestead promoters. It didn't take long for reality to set in. A few figured out how to make it work, but most are long gone. We'd rather blame the promoters selling dreams to people who had nothing. We'd rather not consider the people who were already here, don't you think? And you're challenging something really basic about how we relate to the land. It may well be a challenge we need to hear, but I don't think it makes you a lot of friends in Harstad."

Now I was preaching when I would rather hear Joe say something about Harstad life in 1918. Before he could respond to my observation, I asked Joe, "Your forebears came to this region, speaking German. They had a family and sectarian heritage that resisted military conscription. When the US entered the First World War against Germany, how did they react? More to the point, how did the whole community react?"

Joe tapped his cigarette on the ashtray, took another puff, and said into the exhaled smoke, "First you say you need to wrap this up, then you ask enough for me to go on all day. I'll try for brief, but don't count on it. Before the war German was just one of the immigrant languages, of course. Country schools often taught in the language of the children's families. There were pockets where everyone was German, or Norwegian, whatever. But as the war dragged on in Europe, it got more tense around here for the German speakers. English speaking people, the majority, started to pay more attention to the cultural differences. Their prejudices came out of hiding and into the open. Our folks were accused of being pacifists—why is that a dirty word to so many Christians?"

"I don't know." I answered a question intended to be merely rhetorical. "As one who is both a Christian and a pacifist, I wonder about that, too."

Joseph didn't let himself get sidetracked. "Even worse than that, they were accused of being pro-Kaiser, without any real current evidence. So, when America entered the war there were some young men who thought they could change it by joining the army. Others went as draftees. I guess that either the history of draft-resistance—I don't think it was ever as big a deal as some now claim—either it had been forgotten, or they were more American than anything else, really. By then the young adults were bi-lingual—German at home and English in the high school and town.

"As far as the attitude of the community as a whole? Well, I've about said it. There was a change—I'm giving you my sense of it from my reading and talking to folks. There was a change from a self-identity as Odessa German to American of German descent. They or we didn't want to be the foreigners welcomed by the powers, a people who can be easily exiled by those same powers. Even the churches were beginning to have some of their programs in English at that time."

"You've kind of confirmed some of what I suspected, and added some more insights," I said. "Now I really do need to get going. You'll have to guide me to your house."

Joe insisted on paying for my breakfast, so I left a tip that held the extra coffee and attention in mind. Joe directed us to his house in a sub-division about a mile out of town that I didn't know existed until then. Along the way he played tour guide, pointing out landmarks with historical significance or general interest—several that I'd frequently gone by without noticing.

17

The stimulating conversation and coffee overload of the morning should have been all the energizer I would need to complete my sermon preparation for the following Sunday. Instead it seemed to provoke a writer's block. I started several times, and several ways, and could not find a satisfactory way to fit the scripture with our talk of relationship to the land.

On Sunday morning I still didn't really have a handle on what I should say to share Gospel with the congregation of expectant believers and seekers. We ended up with a mishmash of ideas about relationships, of being first or last, or first with childlike acceptance. The land that holds us became just one more metaphor in my feeble attempts to articulate our relationship with the divine wholeness. Before I stepped down from the pulpit I almost apologized for my ramblings.

As people passed through the open double doors from worship center to front hallway most shook my hand with a non-committal good morning. Madge reminded me, "I'm the oldest, you know," but several people had comments that indicated that they were really touched by something along the way. I guess the sermon heard can be more than the sermon preached, after all.

Berta and I enjoyed our Sunday lunchtime debriefing. As usual, Berta pointed out what I might have said better, along with the reminder that she might have missed most because the girls were as active as ever. I could admit my lack of a clear point, but also point out that some heard something they needed to hear anyway. By the time I'd stretched out on the sofa and slept through most of a televised football game, I was ready to pursue my investigations about the happenings of 1917-18 without bothering to consider how it might be preached. It finally hit me that my history study was part of learning the local mores and traditions. After trying to fit the things I was hearing into the message I was proclaiming as the preacher, I remembered what I had been told before I arrived, that one should learn how the local folks function, learn their mores, before you try to change anything.

The immediate translation of that bolt from the blue would begin that evening in the church basement. The focus would be on the local mores and ways of our teenagers as they made plans for youth group activities with their new adult guides. I was pleased to see that Stephanie was present. I was even more pleased at her suggestion to the group. The young people brainstormed ideas for activities, fun events and fund raising to pay for the fun. It was Steph who got the others to think about projects to help others. By the time they were done they had planned events that alternated between programs that were for themselves and activities to help others. Madge and Nilda, along with all the other Prairie Manor dwellers would see some new visitors soon.

That evening, after the youth meeting, I made some sketchy notes in my journal. I needed two pages, to keep the kids and the history separate. I put down a few reminders of the local history discoveries I'd made, along with the open questions. It was no surprise that at the center of my open questions was getting at the details of this thing they call the killing.

***

As I emerged from sleep on Monday morning, my first thoughts took me right back to the notes I had made the evening before. More than anything I wanted to pry the whole story out from Madge's memories. As soon as the idea of marching right over to Prairie Manor and asking the question until I could get an answer popped into my head, I saw how foolish that idea was. Madge set her own pace, and there would be no way to hurry it.

Just back off, look for information in other places on this day. If Madge lives long enough, she will tell me what happened. That was a sobering thought. It hit me that Madge, well into her nineties, seemed to have less energy at our last couple of visits.

I decided to spend my morning on some overdue household chores and visit the library in the afternoon. In mid-afternoon I walked over and found the library locked up tight: Closed on Columbus Day. I could either get back to my fretting about what Madge and Nilda still wouldn't quite tell me, or I could force myself to set it aside for the day. Both Madge and Nilda sure seemed to keep me aware of what they were not telling me by repeatedly coming to the edge of it. Still, I was mostly able to set it aside and think about other things. This lasted for three whole days. On Tuesday I joined the singers, but intentionally avoided my habit of arriving early for visits.

18

It was Wednesday afternoon by the time I tried the library door again. School had dismissed for the day a few minutes earlier. I should have remembered that all the students would be out at kindergarten dismissal time before the no-school days ahead. It was the reason we weren't starting our Wednesday Church School sessions until the following week. I held the door for several noisy latch-key kids arriving with their heavy book bags. All the kids were of that in-between age—too old for day care but too young to be left alone at home. Sophie directed the young folks to tables, encouraged a somewhat lower noise level and suggested some activities more appropriate to the library. Then she turned to greet me.

"Hi there, Rev," she said, "what can the Kirchen County Library do for you today?"

"Oh, you know," I replied, "the same. I'm still trying to find out what happened in 1918. I know the year at least. What Madge or Nilda talk around but never about. Coming here now, I'm wondering about something else, too. Is this after school program anywhere near your job description?"

"Well, no, not as such, Wil. But I really don't mind, and we do have afternoon volunteer library help."

"But seven kids with energy to burn, who've just come from being cooped up in school. Does Harstad need to organize an after school program? Or the church do more than our once a week that only begins next week?"

"Seven is not typical," Sophie said. "It's the early out, today. There are usually just three or four regulars, so I wouldn't worry about it yet. I say that, because I'm coming to the conclusion that Harstad doesn't plan ahead for what might come. They only react when a problem smacks them in the face."

"Is that what you really think? We know that pipeline crews are coming next year," I said. "That'll mean more kids for a time. And they might hire support staff, putting more moms on the job at this time of day. Don't you think we might anticipate and be ready?"

"Nope. You know I haven't been here much longer than you, but I've seen how things go. Why do you think your youth group sponsors are the new couple in town, and not those who could say, 'We tried that before. It didn't work'? And before was probably a whole generation earlier."

"Maybe you're right. But hey, speaking of youth group, Stephanie helped change the whole character of their planning the other night. She made a suggestion that some events should be to help other people, and they ran with it. Their planning turned from teen fun club into a Christian service group—and teen fun club, too, we hope. After she opened them to service projects, they even decided to take turns leading devotional time at the meetings. And they even signed up. You have a bright, kind, generous and fun-to-be-around kid, Sophie."

Sophie was peeking around my shoulder to something behind me as I finished that.

"Hi, Steph," she said then. "Reverend Wil was just talking about you. Did you hear him?"

"Yeah," Stephanie said, without emotion, with only a nod toward me. "I heard. There's no reason to start on homework tonight. Can I go on home?"

"There are more grade school kids here than usual. Could you just see how those two little girls over in the corner are getting on? I gave them some puzzles, but I haven't seen them here before. Could you, just while I help Reverend Wil for a couple minutes." Sophie pointed to a table nearly hidden by non-fiction stacks. "Then you can go. Okay?"

"Okay, but then I can go, right?"

"That's what I said." As Stephanie left earshot, Sophie added quietly, saying it with a laugh, "Takes compliments well, doesn't she."

"It's an awkward age. But so is thirty-five like me, and so are eighty and ninety-something, too." Assuming Sophie was picking up on my thoughts, I said, "They just can't quite tell me what happened in 1918. So, I'm hoping maybe we can still find some information. Just enough to ask the right leading questions, even. Madge hasn't really talked about the First World War, but that seems to be a biggie for Nilda," I continued, ready to go on.

Sophie stopped me, saying, "I really haven't been able to locate records that tell us anything. Have you asked at the newspaper?" She didn't wait for an answer. "I haven't given up asking the older library users, though. On a whim I tried this: I'll open the conversation by asking about their ethnic heritage, and only after they share a bit of that do I ask anything about life in the 'teens' decade. Everybody is proud of their heritage, but what I see is that the English, Scots and Norwegians were mixing and intermarrying earlier than the Germans. It seems like that's part of the tension of that time. What's cause and what's effect is a whole other question, though, isn't it. Germans were trying hard to prove their patriotism, but they stayed German. Of course, I haven't even considered the Catholic and Protestant divide in this."

"Interesting," I said, "but we don't know, and may never figure out, whether it was the religious heritage that kept German ethnicity more pronounced, or the way they were set apart because of the war against their ancestral home."

Changing the subject only slightly I continued, "I'm not sure of any of this, but it looks like the League leadership wasn't dominated by any one ethnic group, but the Norwegian farmers sure joined up. But that may be just because they were a dominant group among the North Dakota homesteaders."

Sophie took the subject back, "Folks other than German often want to tell me about their own heritage and also that of their spouses. They want me to know how American their children are. I think that's true among the German in the next generations, the ones born about that time and since. I ask about World War One, like I told you before, and it doesn't seem to matter what they've told me about their heritage, they want to move the talk to the family members who served in World War Two."

I said, "I guess I knew that I didn't come to the library for the books today. You're making some intriguing discoveries about our neighbors. I begin to believe that something happened here in 1918 that was supposed to settle a score. If it worked, wouldn't people be willing to talk about it?"

The noise level in the room was going up again. It looked like some young people would need Sophie's attention, so I wrapped up our talk, saying, "Your stern glare at the kids isn't having an effect. You better talk to them, and I'll be on my way."

"Good to talk with you, Rev. We're meeting some friends in Bozeman this weekend, so we'll probably see you Sunday after next."

"You'll miss Jeanine's Laity Sunday sermon, then. I hear she's ready and willing to be more controversial than I am."

As I left I noticed that Stephanie was still there with the two girls, who appeared to be seven or eight. She was helping them choose books to check out. They all seemed happy in their quest. I think I heard her recommend books by Beverly Cleary about Beezus and Ramona Quimby. I knew that there was one copy of *Ramona the Pest* that they wouldn't find. It was at our house, being read a chapter each night with our Ruthie.

19

Cal was already emptying his first or second cup of coffee when I arrived at the Hilltop Café at 6:25 Friday morning. The others—Sherm, Ed, Gary, and Karl—followed within a few minutes. I greeted Cal and said, "You're early. You didn't convince Joseph to come again?"

"Joe said he might be along, but it sounded like he had some project today. I think we will see him again, though. But a word of caution: If he gets the idea that we expect him to come to church on Sundays, we won't see him on Friday either."

"I sure enjoyed hearing his different perspective last week: his ideas about the dominance of the land under us, and all that. A lot to think about—too much, actually, when I made the mistake of trying to include it in my sermon."

"You don't need to apologize," Ed said, as he sat down. "I liked it. Maybe it wasn't anything you said, but something in it had me thinking about times when I've felt closest to God. And the smell of the soil after a rain is always part of those times."

Then Sherm chimed in, "Does that mean that for Ed you're going to preach a dirty sermon this week, then?"

Cal squirmed, and said, "Even worse. Wil isn't preaching. Jeanine didn't go to Teachers' Convention this year, because she's at home pacing with her yellow pad. My scientist wife is fixing to talk about evolution for Laity Sunday. Which you should know. Aren't some of you helping with the service?"

Sherm replied, "Well, I did know she's preaching, of course. As Diaconate chair, I'm the one who's been recruiting you all to help, haven't I. I expected some science from the science teacher. But evolution?"

"Yep, but with her Christian beliefs, too," Cal said. "She said her topic would be 'God is true, evolution is fact'."

While I could be gratified that a member might say something helpful about that subject, I also worried whether I'd be left trying to put the worms back in the can. The church folks called themselves conservative, but I still wasn't sure just what they meant by that. They seemed mostly a practical bunch who resisted ideologies."

While Sally was pouring our coffee, Gary seemed ready to tell his joke of the week. It was clear that he wanted Sally to hear it. "I think Sally has decided that I should take the brunt of her kidding," Gary said, "so I have to tell you guys about a time I was eating lunch in here last summer. A man and woman from out of town came in and sat in that corner booth. When Sally came with menus, they asked her to turn the air conditioning up, because they were so hot. She nodded and headed around the counter. When she came back for their order they asked her to turn it down. They were getting cold. Every time they could get her attention they wanted it changed some way or other for about half an hour. I take a long lunch sometimes, so I saw it all. Finally, when they left I asked Sally why she didn't just tell them where to get off. She said, 'It's no big deal. We don't have AC here.' We can count on her to take just as good care of us, see."

"Come on, Gary. That never happened," Sally said.

To which Gary retorted, "Yeah. But it could have."

Sally gave up and took our breakfast orders. The Hilltop had a special that day that was popular with our group. With no wives watching to warn us about what all that gravy does to men's hearts, it was mudslides of biscuits and sausage gravy all around.

I heard Ed at the other end of the table tell Karl, "Good to see you back, Karl. Did you have a good trip?"

"Well, yes we did. We did some ocean fishing out there."

I asked, "Where did you go, Karl?"

"Once the harvest is all done and settled up, we always like to go to Canada for a couple weeks. Frieda's brother is out in British Columbia," he said.

"The harvest is in, you say? What harvest? It's was so dry. You guys have been telling me about nothing growing since we got here in early June."

Karl just kind of mumbled, without answering audibly.

Then Ed said what he thought Karl wanted to keep to himself, "He got his harvest from the Ag Department. Most of us got some disaster payments on our farms this year."

The big smile on Sherm's face was supposed to tell us to take it as a joke, when he grumbled, "Socialists."

The farmers were not amused, so I tried to calm the situation. I turned to Sherm and said, "Where did you have that doctor check-up the other day? When your back was so sore?"

"You know the answer, Wil. At the VA in Miles City. I'm a vet. I earned that."

"I agree. But it is just as socialist, or none of it is. We're all in it together, in a way. Isn't it in all of our interest to make sure that the guys providing the food and fiber can keep doing it? Just like it's in all our interest to take care of vets?"

"I didn't mean anything by it. Just a little joke, sorry," Sherm said.

"I'm still curious about the real socialists and the those against them back in the early days around here. Gary," I said between bites, "the local information at the library only goes back to about 1928 or '29. Oh, and I know there's some family history stuff that started being compiled back before the town's golden anniversary. So, I ask you, does the Harstad Herald have archives of newspapers from the early days?"

Gary answered, "I'm not sure what all there is on the moldy basement shelves over there. I'll ask the boss. You're asking about socialists in particular?"

"Well, that and about a death, a killing in 1918. I'm still not sure if that even happened in Montana, but I'm starting to suspect it did," I said.

Cal jumped up as he so often did, leaving in a rush to be on time for work. That started the exodus of the whole group. I left thinking I'd opened another can of worms, stirring trouble from my own use of the term 'socialism'. My non-ideological conservatives sure didn't want to be tarred with a leftist ideology. Which would raise hackles more—that or Jeanine's Sunday talk?

20

I found Ruthie and Becca eating dry cereal while watching Sesame Street, and Berta in the basement starting a load of laundry when I got home. The talk at breakfast about archives and even the mentions of socialism had local history intruding on my thoughts again. Without a sermon to prepare, it might be a good time to consider what I was learning in a more orderly way. I put on a warm sweater, grabbed my journal, told the family I'd be at the office, and headed there on foot.

Opening the journal, which was just wire bound notebook, I turned through pages of sketchy notes, best efforts at verbatim transcripts from Madge and Nilda conversations, to do lists and 'ponderisms'. On the first blank page I made three columns, drawing two vertical lines. My first distraction thought, before I could even write the headings, was 'should've used a straight edge.' I headed the columns: what I think I know, questions about what I've heard, and what I need to know more about. Then, off in the left margin (I discovered I needed another column) I wrote on the heading line, 'About' and below, 'NPL'. I skipped several lines and wrote, 'WW1', and further down the page, 'Killing'.

Then I sat and stared at my page for a long time without writing a thing. Wondering, "What do I actually know about any of this?" I realized that I'd been hearing a lot about family struggles and joys, with mentions along the way of wider world issues. It occurred to me that we measure our lives in the personal relationships. I had been thinking that it was the League and then added the war, the issues behind the struggles that would be the key to understanding my task.

I turned to the next blank page and converted these thoughts into journal notes. Writing them down helped me see that my quest was yet to learn what really happened in either Kirchen or Sage County in 1918, because whatever happened back then still resonated among my friends. I turned back to my page of columns, and wrote in the lower right corner, under questions, in the killing section, 'What really happened?'

"Okay," I said to the empty, still chilly office, "that's a start." So, I went down to the church kitchen and started brewing a half-pot in the Mr. Coffee. By the time I got back, mug in hand, to the page-staring contest, I knew that understanding the larger issues of a political prairie fire and a war against Germany and its central powers alliance were important for understanding the more personal and family struggles.

Down at the bottom of my page, on the last line in the first column I wrote, 'it is important.' Then I forced myself back to the top of the page, pen in hand, ready to write, if I had a clue, what I really know, question or need. I put the pen down, wandered down the stairs, refilled my coffee mug, plodded back up to the office with a few thoughts ready to commit to writing.

I wrote:

NPL in 1918—

• Rising fast in ND. Using the primary elections of both Republican & Democratic parties, mostly Rep., to field their candidates. Electing many that Nov. Tight control of voting—to come in 1919 legislature.

• A presence in MT as a new party. With some promise, but not electing beyond local. B.K. Wheeler will (when was this?)..., then become D.

• Organized opposition making noise in both states.

War hysteria—

• Sedition/treason accusations aimed at many with NPL connections. Socialist philosophy, IWW, NPL got lumped together in many people's minds by opposition groups' literature in Mont – NoDak it was direct accusations at NPL.

• Question – how did war hysteria, the sedition and treason accusations at those who supported neutrality affect NPL organizing? Weren't they often accused of anti-war sentiments? Were accusations valid? NPL still growing in NoDak, tho. NPL goals of state owned grain elevators and grading, state bank for farm loans, being accomplished. Control of Republican Central Committee.

• Does success in NoDak mean opposition more effective and strident in Montana? I think so. How does this play out in Kirchen Co.?

• Question – how does the 'killing' connect to any of this?

• I know that Elwin was NPL, and a freelance organizer.

• I know that Walter Ruud was in Europe at least until the Armistice (do I really know this?) I do know that Nilda was living with her parents in spring/summer 1918.

Soon I had little notes scattered all over the page, until my columns and sections meant nothing, and it was a challenge to decipher anything I had written. Near the bottom of the page, across two columns, I wrote: I need to know the details of the killing. Why do I think I must know about it?

After I'd written that final scribble across my page, I sat, leaning back in the swivel chair, feet on desk, remembering Berta's first reaction when I recounted an early conversation with one of my elderly friends. She didn't think it should be my job to explore such long ago events. At the time I defended it as pastoral care to help Madge (it was Madge, wasn't it?) be reconciled with it. As I pondered, I had to question my motives again. So far Madge was unable to talk about the specific event, but otherwise seemed to be a happy, well-adjusted elder. Nilda, on the other hand, was tormented by something, and had battled depression—either long ago, or for a lifetime. So, maybe the need to get Madge to tell me was more pastoral care for Nilda, then. Besides, if it is only my curiosity getting the better of me, then it is abetted by Berta's curiosity now, too. And Cal's. And Sophie's.

Feet on the desk, leaning back in the swivel chair, I was snoozing when the phone rang. I jumped out of my nap, and answered on the third ring forgetting where I was, "Hello, um, Community Church. This is Pastor Wilson."

At the other end of the line Berta said, "Were you asleep?"

"I was pondering, and questioning my motives about finding out what happened in 1918. I just dozed off for a minute," I claimed. It had actually been closer to twenty minutes.

"Then you're all rested up. Are you about ready for some lunch? Frieda called. She and Karl would like us to come to lunch with them at the Hilltop. We'll pick you up in about fifteen minutes, if that's okay."

"I'm ready. I'll be listening for the roar of the Renault. Are you sure you can tolerate a whole mealtime of Frieda?"

"Well, they're buying for all of us. I'll sure try. See you in a few."

We rang off. I took another long look at my journal notes. I made a few notes on the next page, a page that I had started on earlier, about what the next steps might be to satisfy my curiosity. I closed the notebook, took my mug downstairs, shut off and emptied the last of the coffee into the sink, and went out to wait and watch for Berta and the kids.

21

At the café we found Karl and Frieda waiting at the big table where Karl and I had eaten breakfast just a few hours earlier. Menus and kid's coloring pages were set out for us. We took our seats and got the kids settled. We even let Becca convince us that she's really too big for a booster—expecting that she'll change her mind when the cheese sandwich and chocolate milk come and are hard to reach. We opened menus, but before I could consider the choices, Karl gave the table two quick taps with his fingers, and said, "It isn't socialism, you know."

"What?....oh....this morning," I sputtered. "What isn't socialism, then?"

"Sherm called disaster relief socialism, and I didn't think that was a funny joke. Did you? I couldn't tell—were you defending us farmers, or were you defending socialism? Where would farming, and his job, too, be without some relief when there's almost no crop? We pay big in taxes and we insure what can be insured, and the Ag payments aren't really that much. Not enough to pay for a little vacation and still keep farming. It wasn't the government that paid for our trip, whatever Ed and Sherm say."

"My goodness, Karl," Frieda said. "I'm sure nobody meant

you no harm. What does it matter what Sherm says. He's always trying to get somebody's goat. Can't you just ignore it?"

"No, Frieda," Karl nearly shouted. Next he'll be calling me a commie. I won't have it. I think it starts with all that talk about the Nonpartisan League that Cal and Pastor keep bringing up. I sure don't want to see a repeat of the troubles my father went through to keep farming in Kirchen County."

I was about to ask, 'what troubles?' when the teenage waitress, working during the school break, came to take our lunch orders. A strong family resemblance told me that she was Sally's daughter. And Sally came right behind her with crackers for the children. So I was reminded of our little girls' presence with us. If Karl really meant troubles in the way he said the word, maybe I didn't want him to describe them here. In any case, 'socialism' seemed to be a dirty word devoid of any real meaning for Karl. That's probably the way most of the Harstad guys used the word.

Instead, I tried to shift to more pleasant talk, "The British Columbia coast sounds like a nice place to visit in the fall. Did you bring home some big fish?"

"Frieda and the sister-in-law did better fishing the tourist shops. The sea was rough to where we didn't do much catching and hardly fished, really. But once we got back on solid ground, the beer was good. I'll say that for those Canadians," Karl said. "I have to tell you how it is that we can take our trips. I don't like to mention this to the preacher, don't you know. You'll think we should give even more to the church than we already do. It's not the farm or the government that buys a trip. It's what's under the farm. We have a couple producing wells on some acreage where we still have the oil and gas rights. So, we have some steady income 'til the wells dry up or they cap them. And the church does get its share, so don't get any ideas."

"I really don't know how much anyone gives. I'm not sure I even want to."

"Well Wil, you're young. You don't know if it would make a difference how you treat people if you knew what they give. Stick around long enough and you'll know who gives even if you never see the books. There's lots of things, and not just money—lots of things you never get told about. Some stuff you just have to figure out about us."

I didn't know how to respond to that statement, so I didn't. Calmly advising me about my congregation showed that Karl's anger had been released. In the pause with Karl I noticed that another conversation was going on beside us. Berta was looking agitated and not saying much. Our burgers and the kids' cheese sandwiches arrived, so she was able to turn her attention to the children. I had not managed to hold to my intention that I would find ways to deflect Frieda's annoying habit of giving Berta unwanted and unneeded instructions on how to be a proper minister's wife. Now it was done and I hadn't even heard her comments. If it was too late to come to the defense of my wife, could it possibly help her feel better if I stirred things up with Karl again? If I had given it any real thought, I'd have remembered why I didn't want to hear about 'troubles' and stopped myself.

I swallowed the first big bite of my hamburger and said, "Karl, you haven't objected to the talk about the NPL at our breakfasts, but now it sounds like that's been a sore spot for you. What's that all about?"

"Preacher, there are things besides our tithes that you don't want to get into," and having said that, Karl paused. Then he took a deep breath. Frieda was busying herself with ketchup. For the moment, the only sound from our group was Becca kicking the underside of the table from the booster seat she had accepted at last.

Finally, Karl went on, "There are things....It was a long time ago, but some folks still remember. I was just a little boy, but I remember some of the talk. Mostly what I remember growing up after those times, was how people kept leaving. It was politics when I was too young to understand any of it. Not long after it seemed like everybody was pulling together. It didn't matter so much anymore if your accent was Deutsch or Norski or even Polish. What mattered was how much longer you could stay and farm."

Frieda interrupted Karl, saying with her accent of a slight by unmistakable hint of German, "Ya, he says it don't matter so much. That's compared to that first war time when it mattered way too much. Before that time it mattered where you come from. That's how my mother talked about it. Then when America went to war against the Kaiser, it was 'Germans can't be trusted.' They figured us German folk must be loyal to the Kaiser, even though our ancestors had been in Ukraine for a hundred years. And they didn't think the Norwegians was patriotic enough. They was all pegged as NPL socialists and pacifists, no matter what they really might've been. So first it'd be where you was from. Then it divided up the native born against the immigrants, you see. Then it got all confused, too, don't you see, 'cause there was so many of the League leaders trying to poke their nose into Montana politics. Don't matter that they're American just as far back as the other troublemakers. Troublemakers all of them, I say."

Karl waited through Frieda's interruption, then continued as if it hadn't happened. "Friends kept disappearing from the land in those days. You talk about how dry this year was, well let me tell you something, I've seen dry. And I've seen real radicals—socialists and communists and Wobblies—stirring up trouble, using the people, taking advantage of their desperate situation. It's a thing like disaster payments that saves the republic, I believe. Maybe that's all the League really wanted, but that's sure not the way they remember it here. And things settled down after 1918, until the dry years pushed so many off the land. And it's about to happen again. We can get better crops out of less moisture here that just about anywhere, but now we have to learn how to farm Wall Street, too. And that means we're seeing a new kind of dry. Wall Street is farming us, I'm afraid."

"That's some deep stuff to consider, Karl," I said. But I didn't have the heart to say what I was thinking—that he was starting to sound like a Nonpartisan League organizer. 'Wall Street' sounded a lot like 'Big Biz'. I did ask, though, "What do you think got the Ag Department into the kind of support system we have now? Could it have been League activism that's behind some of it? Or does it really start with FDR? Or what?"

"Roosevelt was one to warn about the dangers of communist

tyranny, don't you see. You might say it was a compromise, government support and not government takeover. Maybe the noise they made in North Dakota in those early days was inspiration. I just have to think that what's coming now is another thing entirely. I just hope those wells keep producing. I'm too old to change." With that, Karl ended his speech.

Someone in a booster seat was indicating that she really needed to be taken home and put down for a nap, so we said our thank you and good bye, as Karl attacked the French fries he'd neglected because he had so much to say.

***

Late that afternoon I once again opened my journal. I looked first at the chart page I had set up in the morning. Was there anything that Karl or Frieda had said that adds to what I know? He had hinted at something that affected the relationships among ethnic groups locally. I quickly abandoned the chart, opened the next page to add a couple new notes.

• Is it true? Progression from tensions among immigrant groups (all northern European, of course), to 2-way tension between immigrants and 'already American' homesteaders, to all against the drought/economic conditions driving them off the land.

• Karl and Frieda have interesting way that they handle each other's interruptions. Karl just waited while Frieda talked, then went on from where he left off. He hardly acknowledged what she'd added.

• What caused relations to change? In the time before and after WW1 from politics (political divisions?) to pulling together? Such that even a young child noticed? Was it the war? Sounded like something more local, but he was young, as he said. Surely it wasn't....no.

• Berta didn't say anything about any nonsense Frieda was giving her, ..had her bristling. I probably should ask, but then again...

Since my journaling was getting far afield, it was time to let it go. I closed the notebook, ready for some family time.

22

Ruthie and Becca came to church with me on Sunday morning. Berta sent us off challenging me to deal with our daughters through an hour of church for once. I was ready to enjoy leadership and presentations from others, hoping the girls would let me. When we arrived, it came as a surprise to learn that I was still expected to play a master of ceremonies role. Seeing to the children wasn't too difficult, after all. Mary Ann and Henry supervised them through much of the hour.

I had high hopes for Jeanine's sermon and it was better yet. She articulated her personal faith well, sharing what Christ means to her. She spoke of ways creation and life go on changing, that is evolving, and how her faith is deepened in the midst of a universe that seems both random and incredibly creative. I should have taken notes, but I was sitting with my kids and good neighbors for that part of the service.

23

On the following Tuesday afternoon I headed for Prairie Manor early enough for a visit with either Nilda or Madge, but not both. As I approached the entry I was thinking, 'I wonder if there's another way in. I really want to talk with Madge, but Nilda will be laying for me with that four-footed cane ready to strike.' All the other outside doors seemed to be equipped with alarms to alert staff to anyone going out, so I strode on through the main door. And what luck, Nilda was nowhere in sight. Then the worry entered my mind, and a brief prayer—hope she's okay.

I found Madge in the main room, plodding slowly behind her walker toward her favorite spot. The central area of the room was open enough that her elbows and dancing walker couldn't fill it the way they did the church aisle, but it looked like she was trying, and very nearly succeeding.

I stepped over to Madge, turning with the intention of walking beside her and helping her get seated, and said, "Hello, Madge. How are you this afternoon?"

The bright sun beating through the big south windows was in our faces as she looked over at me. I quickly regretted my deliberate greeting without the usual re-introduction. Either the sun, her memory, or both kept her from recognizing.

"Is there something you want, sir? Are you the doctor?" she asked.

I had another chance, "The sun is blinding us, I think. I'm Pastor Wil. I thought we might visit for a few minutes, if that suits you."

"Oh, Pastor Wil. Of course." And she reached out her right hand, pulling me closer to the walker, and gave a sort of sideways hug. "Come sit down. Over in the corner, there."

As Madge got settled in her favorite chair, I went across to borrow a chair from one of the round dining tables. As I did, a frail looking woman whom I could not remember having seen before, pushed close in her wheelchair, blocking my path. She looked up at me, pointed across the room to Madge, and said, "She says she's the oldest, but she's not."

I replied, "Pleased to meet you. I'm Pastor Wil, from the Community Church."

"She's not, I tell you," she repeated.

"Oh, who is?"

"What's that you said? I can't hear you. She says she is, but she's not." And with that, she nudged her wheelchair along, shuffling her feet along the floor, to the table where I'd just removed the chair. I just shook my head, carried the chair over to Madge's corner, sat down and opened the stenographer's notebook I'd brought along.

"What's that old biddy telling you, Pastor?" she asked.

I think she knew, but I only said, "Just saying hello, mostly. But hey, you've been telling me about Elwin and how he helped the League and all. Is there anything more you want to remember today?"

"I might not be the oldest in town, but at church I'm the oldest, you know."

"I do know that. And one of the best, too."

"I see you brought paper and pen this time. That's good. I was remembering how we relied on the RFD at our North Dakota farm. Three days every week the mailman came. Gunnar Bjerke was his name. We all called him Jerky, but it was his little truck that was the jerky one."

I had started jotting a few notes, but I looked up and saw the smile that reached Madge's eyes when she said, "I think he might've been Norwegian. When his tin lizzie truck was broke down, which it was real often, he'd come on horseback. He'd put the mail in the box about a half a mile up the road. Ours and the Bjornson's boxes were there at the junction corner. If Elwin was out in the field he would be watching for Jerky, hoping for the next issue of the Nonpartisan Leader. It came out once a week, but Elwin would look for it every mail day, regardless. I'd send one of the youngsters down to the box if they weren't all at school or out working with their pop. I told you about selling my eggs, didn't I? How I paid the NPL dues and all?"

"Yes, Madge. You really do have a good memory," I said.

"For an old lady, you were about to say. You can't deny it," Madge insisted with a laugh, and got back to her story telling. "If I had eggs—I was keeping a sizeable flock of chickens by then, what with supplying the NP train, and all—if I had eggs and Elwin was busy on the farm, I'd be watching out and listening for Jerky Bjerke and the mail. I had to get out to the road with my eggs so he'd see me coming and wait. He'd deliver them to the spur at Sage City for us, weeks we didn't get to town. And you know the odd thing about that? Paying the mail to deliver the eggs, I'd end up with about the same amount of money as I got when Elwin took them to town. I thought I knew the exact price they were paying, but I guess Elwin must have got a little more. I think he used it for a schooner of beer after his business was done. He never drank so as to worry me though. One glass to wash out the dust, and he'd come on home, I truly believe.

"The RFD was a real blessing for the farmers, wasn't it," I said. "And I remember that junction you never told me about. I took the wider road and it got me to Sage City just fine."

"You're smarter than you look, so it worked out. That's why they call it Sage City Road," she said, and returned to her reminiscing. "It wasn't long after Elwin died when the mail started coming every day. Elwin would grab the latest Leader issue when he came in for dinner, or before supper if the mail was late. He'd read every word, including all the advertisements. I wouldn't even open it. Only after Elwin read it all, then I would read it, too. As I read, what Elwin hadn't already read to us all, it would worry me more and more. Elwin would read that rag over again all week until the next one came. By the third or fourth time through, he'd be reading most of it out loud. Buddy was getting to be at that rebellious age, and he'd razz his father. 'Pop,' he'd say, 'why do you want to believe all that happy horseshit?' and I'd get after him for his language. Elwin would get after him for questioning his father and for upsetting his mother."

I started to laugh but Madge went on. "Of course Buddy only did it to rile us both. He was really a good boy, nearly a man. Soon enough, he'd have to be the man. That's when I came to consider it this way: It's shit, but it ain't happy and it ain't just road apples, neither."

I swallowed my laughter, even as Madge let out a little giggle. Then, when Madge noticed that I was scribbling in my notepad, she reached over and tried to grab my pen.

"Don't you be writing that part down, Mister. Maybe I was wrong to tell you to take notes. Don't you write that. I don't talk that way, so just forget that, see."

"It was fun, though, wasn't it—to let your son have his say as a teenaged kid, even now," I said. "Thank you for letting him use his own words. See. I'm scratching it all out." I drew a single line through what I'd written. I still wanted to be able to read it. That seemed to satisfy Madge. Once again, though, Madge had made an oblique reference to 'the killing'. When would I ever learn the whole story? I looked at my watch and saw that the singers would be arriving soon and Madge had more to say about the League's newspaper.

"We would listen while Elwin read the parts of the Leader that he wanted us to know about. But he wouldn't tell it all.

After he headed out to the barn—did you see any sign of the barn when you went out there?"

"No. You didn't even mention a barn before."

"Well, I didn't expect you to see anything. They pulled it all out of there just like the house. They plowed that patch— fertilized real good there, too. It wasn't much of a barn, but it stored some hay feed, and housed the milk cow and our two plow horses. Elwin would head out there after his breakfast, milk the cow, and then head out to the field, or work on something right there. No matter what time of the year, he'd go out and I wouldn't see him 'til dinner at noon. He always said, even if there wasn't any real work that had to be done right now; he always said if he didn't get up and go to work he might forget to get up at all. Farming was his job and he did it every day but Sunday. The Nonpartisan League became the hunger that drove him, though. He got this peculiar notion that being a farmer should be a paying job. I sure was with him on that idea. So it worried me. When he'd gone off to work and after I had the dishes washed up, the kiddies off to school or busied some way, and we'd tidied the house a bit, then I would sit down with my tea or coffee and read his Nonpartisan Leader. I'd see those cartoons and stories about the awful things being said about the farmers in the League, the threats. That's along with the great victories the League was having, but some of those victories in the big print turned into promises of someday in the small print of the article. It did worry me. What's really coming? They call the farmers, that's most of the people in all of Dakota, they call us Bolsheviks and worse. How will it end, I wondered. How will it end?"

The question was on my lips, ready to ask, "How did it end?" when Rachel and three other women of the singing group bustled in with boisterous greetings to us. I stood up to return my chair to its place and help move the piano. As I said my farewell, I told Madge, "I'll be back and I'm going to ask you, 'How did it end?'"

While we put the piano in its place I remembered that I hadn't seen Nilda. I excused myself and went to her room. She was there, eating cookies, laughing and visiting with Frieda. As we all walked to the big room, Frieda said she'd found Nilda sitting near the front door when she came in earlier, and they just got to visiting for an hour or more.

I asked, "Frieda, are you one of the singers now?"

"Oh no," she said, "I can't hold a note with a co-signer. I just came to listen and visit for a bit."

I took my place among the group, joining another male voice for once. Rachel sat down at the piano and announced to us that Nellie and Matthias had chosen the music this time. They were all songs we might have learned at camp or youth fellowship. We did not sing 'Smiles'.

24

On Thursday morning I was called to come to the Manor to pray and be with the family of a man who was near death. Mr. Johnson and his family were all unknown to me, so I had no idea what to expect. Nilda saw me come in, but didn't interfere with my determined march to the front desk and, with a nurse, to the man's room. She filled me in as we walked down the hall, saying that his children were all there, but were showing some deep tensions with each other. Six people were introduced to me as his sons and daughters, while a few spouses and members of the next generation came in and out. The man did indeed seem close to departing this life, so after a brief and not very informative conversation with two of the daughters we circled the bed and prayed for ease in his transition through death and for the surviving family. Then a son, who looked significantly younger than the others said, "Shouldn't they take dad over to the hospital?"

The daughter who had taken the lead in introductions and our earlier chat reacted, saying, "Ray, we've been through this. There's really nothing to be done."

Just after she said that we were all surprised to hear a croaking voice from the bed. It sounded to me like their dad said "amen."

There was a silence in the room and then a daughter turned to me and said, "Thank you for coming, Pastor." Others nodded, making it clear that they were ready for me to leave them. As I left the room, I wondered whether the 'amen' was to the statement 'nothing to be done' or to silent prayer that continued after mine had ended.

I thought it best to stay nearby for a while, in case they should need something more from me, so I went looking for Nilda. Having had an hour with Madge two days earlier, I was ready to hear some more from Nilda. I found her sitting near the entryway, a spot that was becoming her territory in the same way that the sunny corner was Madge's. The rule makers of Prairie Manor had recently given up on their contention that the doorway was not a place to congregate, and put a few chairs against the wall in the wide hallway. Of course all the chairs were occupied. I told Nilda I'd find a chair, but instead she led me to her room. I let them know at the desk where I'd be if the Johnson family should want me.

***

Nilda and I sat down in our usual places: she in the deep chair and I in the straight back chair facing the window. It still bothered me that this put me so much higher physically. I was constantly aware of the power dynamic that could cause. Nilda seemed able to overcome that by playing the host, while sending me on errands—first to the dining area for two cups of coffee, then to retrieve the shoebox of old snapshot pictures.

Settled in chairs once again, now with a shoebox on my lap, Nilda began by asking, "How is Mr. Johnson? I see all his family around, and it isn't his birthday."

I was slow to answer, wondering how much confidentiality was required. Finally I said, "He's not well. How are you this frosty morning?"

"Oh, is it cold outside? Guess I should get out more."

"I think this morning we had our first really hard freeze, 15 on our thermometer when I got up. I was expecting a solid freeze in September. Does it usually come this late around here?"

"This is kind of late. It makes me sad that I don't bother to get out every day or even notice the weather." A faraway look came over her face as she went on, "The first ice on the dam, when you'd see it reaching around the edge of the pond. That was always an exciting time for me. A change in the season always perked me up, it would make me quit feeling sorry for myself, somehow. Here's to the coming winter." As she spoke, Nilda lifted her Styrofoam coffee cup, so I did the same. I was paying attention to her toast and let the box of photos slide off my knee. A fifty year accumulation of black and white pictures, in great variety of sizes and quality scattered over the floor. I got down on my knees, and handling them as carefully as I could, I began to gather them back to together. I put a few back into the box.

Then Nilda stopped me. Pointing toward the pile, she said, "Let me see that one."

I had no idea which she was asking for, so I handed her several.

"Oh, these bring back memories. Give me that one of Fort Peck." I rummaged a bit, until she gave the right signal, saying, "Yes, that one."

Three or four photos came stuck to that one, so now she had a lapful to look at while I restored the rest to the shoebox. Nilda and her photographs were ready to reminisce.

"Walter took us places. It was not an easy life, you know." She handed me a picture of a dusty, ramshackle street that looked like a set for an old west movie. "That was New Deal, Montana. That was when we were building the Fort Peck Dam. That was one rough boomtown. But there was work for Walter. He was a hard worker. If he could just stay out of trouble with bosses we wouldn't have had to move so much. He wasn't like that when I married him, you know.

"Walt came back from the war, all full of hope for a nice family, so it seemed to me. But there was something different. Maybe melancholy was catching out there. Papa had changed by then, too. All changed by something, and secretive. It was a long time, well not so long, but it seemed so, before I learned what really happened. And then I began to question, you see. Isn't there something I could've done to make it different? It troubles me. Why couldn't I make it better?"

She paused with her question, that wasn't really being asked if me. I didn't try to respond. We waited.

Then Nilda looked again at the pictures she was holding and resumed her reminiscing. "We did travel around a bit. Look at all the places. I took pictures of all the different places. Walter dug holes for REA power poles, ran the big graders to pave the roads. He was always ready to go wherever there was work. And he was too often ready to get away from whatever job he was on at the time. He never talked about what happened in the war, but something over there sure made him have a hard time around people. A little whiskey, another fight and we'd be packing up again. We were awful hungry before the dam work started. No pun intended."

Nilda poked my knee with her forefinger, to let me know the pun was very much intended.

"Look at all those pictures of all the places. I took most of them with my Brownie box camera. Now I look and where are my kiddies? All those pictures to remind me of the places, and not enough of them with my family."

I dug through the box looking for the people pictures. Nilda was right, the places predominated. And the places were mostly of temporary boom towns, trailer camps, and work sites with vast expanses of Montana empty prairie in the background. A few had mountains, fewer still in populated places. I recognized settings in uptown Butte and Great Falls. As I pulled out the family pictures I noticed first that very few showed smiling faces. The only smiles anywhere were on the children and looked like fake 'say cheese' smiles. Without comment, I handed them all to Nilda.

She looked carefully at each one, telling me the ages of Magda and Walter, Jr. and where she thought each picture had been taken. No two were in the same community, at least as she remembered. After she had handed them back to me, one at a time, she asked me to prop them on the sill against the window. She turn and gazed at the row for a moment and said, "We were a stern troop of wanderers, weren't we?"

"But look at the happy faces in those pictures all around your room," I said. "And I don't mean the politicians."

"Well, yes. I'm glad life is better for my great-grandkids," Nilda said. "With Walt's work, or lack of it, our family was always on the move. It didn't make for a happy home life. Maggie and Junior always adapting to a new school, or just missing out entirely. They sure learned their geography, though. Junior would find his way among the boys by getting in fights. Looking back, I suppose that was his way to be like his Papa. Maggie looked inward for company—with her dolls and later her diary. Such a dreamy, solitary child."

"Magda lives here in Harstad now, right?" I asked.

"Yes she does. She married a Lutheran, so they go over there. Yah, she goes to his church and he goes fishing. I'll see that you get to meet her one of these days.

"Now, don't get me wrong about what I was saying about my two Walters. You must be thinking Walt was mean to us. In a way, you'd be right, but he never hit any of us. In fact, he never so much as spanked the kiddies, even when they needed it. He let his anger out by breaking something and stomping off the job. Always got good reports for the next job in spite of it. The bosses would say it's shell shock, and recommend him because he always did good work while they had him. Even so, they couldn't convince him to stay. He just had to move on. Any meanness toward us was just that we had to follow along. We didn't have no choice.

"But then, when the dam was all built, and there was no more work for the survivors, we managed to come back home to Kirchen County and settle here in Harstad. Walt seemed to be settling down by then. Oh, he stomped off a few jobs at Fort Peck, but there were so many crews needing men who had skills and smarts, that he kept being hired into another slot. That or just the passing of time settled him. I recall the payday when he came in telling about a raise in pay. He was so proud. It was the first time he stayed on one job long enough to get what they called a longevity raise. That day we all smiled. And nobody took our picture."

Nilda turned again to look at the pictures in the window. A couple had slipped down on the sill. Setting the shoebox on the bed, I got up and righted them again. By then, Nilda was wiping her teary eyes.

I settled back in the chair expecting Nilda to suggest that we pray, which would signal that our time was over. It would still be a while, though. She had more to tell me. And I still wanted to be available if the Johnson family should call for me.

"Oh, it does take me back. We came back here and Walt finally found a boss he could stay with. He put his construction knowledge to work at the lumber yard. John said all was forgiven. John's my brother, both him and Herbert are gone now. John said we should come back to the ranch, but Walt just couldn't face them or farm work. Junior tried it, though. But he didn't know a thing about farming or handling livestock and nobody wanted the trouble to teach him. He never took orders nor teaching. Papa was long gone, but you'd still feel like he was around on that ranch. All somber and secretive out there. Why couldn't I see a way to stop it from ever happening? That night haunts me, too. It haunts me."

"That night?" I said, as always, trying to prompt some real answers in my quest.

"I was so ready to have Walt home," Nilda said, ignoring my question. "The armistice was declared in November 1918. I remember so well, Maggie'd had her first birthday. I remember thinking, 'now Walt will come back and we can celebrate homecoming like a grand birthday party.' It gave me hope. Then....nothing. When I finally heard from him he still didn't know when he'd come home. It was six months before he even came back to the United States, and then it was two more months. Oh, how I worried. Was there something they weren't telling me? Was he gassed, or injured bad? Why wasn't he home?

"Then, finally, he stepped off that train right here in Harstad. His ma was there, I was there with Papa and Mom, and little Magda of course. Walt came jumping and flying to us, with hugs. He grabbed Magda to him and she cried and kicked. She didn't know her daddy from Adam. His smile, so big like it used to be before the war, just dropped off his face. He put the girl down and they never really warmed to each other after that, not like he would love Junior. I picked Maggie up so she didn't toddle off under the train or something. It was probably a good thing Walt wasn't holding her when the train whistle blew and it let off some steam. The noise made Walt jump like he was coming right out of his skin. We didn't think anything of it right then. It wasn't long, though. His nightmares. My happy-go-lucky groom had changed. He'd wake up in the night pouring sweat sometimes and if I tried to comfort him he'd shake and back away like I was trying to hurt him.

"Mom had been telling me about Papa having bad dreams like that and I didn't really believe her. But something had made my brothers disappear to do their own work on the ranch and stay away from Papa. They were living in a shanty house they threw up at the other side of our spread. So our men, Papa and Walt, they were a pair, let me tell you. So, no surprise, Papa was slow to get at his chores. With Walt there, now Papa could blame him for the work not getting done. Then came the big fight. That wasn't just stomping off, it was knock down fight. It was sure a good thing they weren't anywhere near a gun or a pitchfork. They both lived through it, both of them sadder still. And we hit the road. I hadn't yet even told Walt that we were going to have another baby. Nowadays they tell us it's hormones. All I know is my melancholy came back."

Then Nilda gave her good-bye cue, "I'm tired now, and it's almost dinner time. Will you pray for me?"

While we were saying our parting prayer together, an aide came and stood in the doorway until the amen. She motioned me out to the hallway to tell me that Mr. Johnson had died. She said some of the family wanted me to come back to his room for a moment but others were indicating that they did not want a minister around at all. I made my visit with them as brief as I could, realizing that too much of my presence in that moment would only increase the family tensions. I gave what assurance I could, trying for words that could be accepted by all, entrusting them all to God's care. Needing assurance from God myself, I left Prairie Manor full of family dysfunction in one's remembrance and others' present example. Would there be any way that I could ever be of help to the Johnsons? Could I ever help Nilda with her guilt feelings?

25

Soon enough Friday came around, with its early start for breakfast with the men. While standing in a 6 AM shower my thoughts jumped back and forth between the previous day's events and plans for guiding the men's group. Would I be getting a call from Daryl Berry, the funeral director? Did I want that call, and more struggle with that conflicted Johnson family? I had no idea what the family would be doing, or would expect if I were to lead the funeral. The call hadn't come, and the breakfast would come first.

I recalled the lunch with Frieda and Karl, and Karl's objection to using the group to talk about old days focused around political conflicts. But I also remembered that he needed to talk about those times, and that he had his own insights and that he was troubled about something from that time long past. How might I deal with it this morning?

Do we stay so much in the Bible lesson that we lose sight of any application, or connection to our own experience? That would deny the point of our gathering. But Cal and some would be steering us to politics of the early days.

Do I try to steer it to our time right now, for Karl's sake? Then the thought intruded, "does Karl's reference to 'horror' have to do with Madge's repeated mentions of a 'killing' or to what Nilda said yesterday of 'that night'? Could they all be related somehow? Then I knew that my thoughts were taking flights of fancy and remembered that I was in the shower to wash. As I toweled dry, I also remembered that the Friday Breakfast conversation never went as I planned anyway. I dressed and, before the rest of the family woke up, headed on foot for the Hilltop Café at the bottom of the hill.

***

I managed to arrive on time for our 6:30 breakfast. Chuck and Gary were ahead of me, seated at the big table, talking about a big storm coming our way. Outside the large plate glass windows, others of our group were pulling into the parking lot. The sun was peeking over the eastern horizon in a cloudless blue sky. I was comfortable in a light jacket and they were talking about stormy weather. I pointed out the window and greeted them with, "Nice day now. Guess we better enjoy it while it lasts, huh."

Chuck said, "Ain't that the truth. Lois and I are on our way to Billings this morning. Hope we can beat the storm. Might be okay to get stuck in the big town for a couple days, though."

Ed, who was just hanging his chore-coat and cap on a peg, heard this and asked, "But what about your stock, Chuck. If this turns into the blizzard they're predicting, won't you need to see to the cattle?"

"Oh, they'll be alright. We got them pastured close in already, and the boy's there to spread them some hay. Time he learns what his old man's retirement'll feel like," Chuck said.

Sherm was about to sit down, but noticed that all our coffee mugs were empty. Only Chuck's and Gary's had yet been used, and there was no sign of Sally. He stepped around the counter, grabbed the pot, and served us all, with accusations about what our lousy tips were doing to service. Sally appeared with her

130

order pad and a couple menus (just in case), and said to Sherm, "Even if you guilt them into bigger tips, Sherm, I'm not sharing."

Cal and Joseph came in and we were a full table. But Karl was still missing. 'Should I be concerned about his absence?' I wondered to myself. 'He's not that regular, anyway. And everyone else is here, and that's a nice surprise, so enjoy.' No sooner had I resolved my doubts with these thoughts, that Karl came through the door.

"Well, we're a full assembly today. Good to see you all," I said. "You've got an audience for your joke today, Gary."

Gary shook his head, "I'm dry. I got nothing. Sorry."

"Anyone else, then?" I inquired. I hoped to keep our talk in trivialities as long as I could.

After some hemming and hawing, Joe cleared his throat and said, "A Catholic friend of mine assures me that Father McCarthy told this, so I can tell it on him. Seems the good priest was driving a little erratically. The deputy on patrol pulled him over and spotted a wine bottle wedged between the bucket seats of that Camaro he drives. "Father," he says, "you know that Communion wine belongs at the church. Drinking and driving will lead to trouble."

Father McCarthy replies, "Oh no, officer. That's pure water to quench a thirst. I just used the bottle that was handy."

Deputy asks for the bottle. He sniffs it. Then he pours just a little onto the palm of his hand. Nice concord grape purple. He tastes it and says, "Father McCarthy. This is definitely wine."

And our priest says, "Faith and begorrah, Praise be to God. He's done it again."

There was a momentary lag to catch the reference to Jesus' miracle before the laughs started. Once we settled down again, I said, "A miracle. Ties right in with the Bible reading we're going to hear on Sunday, and also right now. It's a different miracle, from another Gospel, this time in Mark 10 about a blind man.

And they came to Jericho; and as he was leaving Jericho with his disciples and a great multitude, Bartimaeus a blind beggar, the son of Timaeus, was sitting by the roadside. And when he heard that it was Jesus of Nazareth, he began to cry out and say, "Jesus, Son of David, have mercy on me!" And many rebuked him, telling him to be silent; but he cried out all the more, "Son of David, have mercy on me!" And Jesus stopped and said, "Call him." And they called the blind man, saying to him, "Take heart; rise, he is calling you." And throwing off his mantle, he sprang up and came to Jesus. And Jesus said to him, "What do you want me to do for you?" And the blind man said to him, "Master, let me receive my sight." And Jesus said to him, "Go your way; your faith has made you well." And immediately he received his sight and followed him on the way.

After a brief pause, Joe said, "Here's the deal. I've been reading the Bible some the past few days. It's all your fault, you know, Wilford. I was looking at the four Gospels from my particular point of view, with the land and the travels to different places at the center of my thoughts. Anyway, here's the deal. You've got this story about a blind man. Why Jericho? Is it just because that's where they were when it happened, or are we supposed to have enough vision to see something else along with this Bartimaeus guy?"

"Well," I said, "maybe we have to get down to Jericho for the trek up to Jerusalem. I don't want to read into the text too much that might not really be there, but I could. I could say that since the disciples had been contending with one another, jockeying for position with Jesus, that this event at the lowest elevation, with a sightless man who gets to see, and has real vision along with it, and follows Jesus on the way—when all that happens, maybe it's about the destination. Maybe we're supposed to see something new about what will happen up at the capital city, at the higher elevation. Or maybe not so new, but see more clearly what it will mean for us—those who follow along the way a long time after Bart."

"But you don't want to read too much into it, you say. Is all that in my Bible, then?" There were laughing nods around the table as Ed said this.

"*Eisegesis* is what that's called, and I'm doing it for sure," I said.

With some effort, Sherm extended his right leg from the chair to reach in his pocket. He pulled out a quarter, dropped it in the middle of the table and said, "Use words like that and it'll cost you. I'll spot you the price this once."

"Why, thank you Sherm." I said, "Are you sure two bits will cover the price? It is Greek, you know. Means 'Reading in'— putting ideas in instead of drawing them out." I put a quarter from my pocket on top of Sherm's. Then I got back to doing what the Greek word describes. "They were on the way to Jerusalem. Jesus had been telling his friends what was in store for him when they would get there. And they were holding on to their pre-conceived notions about a big victory, of what a godly kingdom would be. I think they still expected to throw out the Romans and take over." I looked around the table and asked, "Are you with me so far?" The response was mostly ambiguous murmurs and nods.

Cal, however, answered while turning around to look at the wall clock, "I'm with you, and I'm going to be late for work." He turned back, still sitting, giving no indication that his usual jump and run was coming.

"I better save something for Sunday's sermon. But, you see, I'm afraid we are often like those disciples Jesus was trying to get through to. We keep our spiritual blinders on and act like the cross and resurrection didn't change anything. I was thinking about what our friends over at Prairie Manor keep trying to tell me, and then avoid saying it. About a man getting killed 60 years ago, and what came of it. I hear about a changed community in some way, and about troubled souls. And I wonder who did what to whom. And I ask, do we still think like the mob on Good Friday, that killing, or, at least, getting rid of one at the center of our problem in some way, will fix something in us?"

"You're laying a heavy burden on us, Preacher," Cal said. "But mostly confusion. And now I really am late for work." This time he dropped some cash on the table for his meal, jumped up and ran for the door, pulling his jacket on as he sprinted to his pickup.

To the others, I said, "Blessings on you all, brothers. I can't promise it'll be any less confusing by Sunday, but I'll keep struggling with my questions, and trust the Holy Spirit for guidance."

I could see that Joe's mind was working, getting ready to offer some question, or maybe even an answer. Others were finishing the last of their coffee and saying their good-byes. The expressions on their faces seemed to vary from 'humbug' to 'confusion' to 'interesting ideas'.

When others had gone, Joe said, "You're messing up some of my ideas about place and the land. Oh, I still think it's a really important part of the whole human story, so I intend to keep reading from that angle. Here's the deal though, I think you are onto something about the way we think that we can get out of our conflicts. Like the faction over in Egypt that killed Sadat the other day. It keeps happening. Do you really think that your killing in 1918 was a scapegoat deal like that?"

"Scapegoat. That's the word I was looking for," I said. "I don't know if that's what went on, but I still intend to find out, if I can."

"Well, if there's any way I can help, let me know," Joe said. "I've got my own wheels today, so I won't be begging a ride. Be seeing you."

"That's good because I walked." I accepted Joe's offer of a ride. As we got into his enormous Olds I realized what I'd forgotten, and said, "I forgot to ask Gary about the archives at the newspaper. Drop me at the Herald office and I'll check up on it. I'm hoping we can find something from '18."

***

At the Harstad Herald, Gary got up from a keyboard, came to the counter and informed me that records before 1925 were lost in a fire, and records from other competing weeklies had never been stored. Since Gary hadn't said anything about it at breakfast, I really didn't expect much. He seemed more disappointed than I. Then he took time to show off the brand new word processing equipment that he had been working at. The Harstad Herald was entering the computer age.

26

By Sunday dusk the snow was beginning to blow past our front window in that western plains way. The snow doesn't fall, we'd decided, it moves horizontally to North Dakota unless there's a structure or a tree in the way. The forecast told us this would be a major storm by morning. It wasn't yet serious enough to cancel our youth meeting. Still, I was surprised to see four high school and three middle school students in attendance—all the town kids and, wisely, none of our farm kids.

Jennifer, who lived on a ranch about twenty miles out, had signed up to lead an opening devotion. Julia, adult co-leader, looked toward me. She was starting to ask that I do that part when LeRoy announced that Jennifer had already asked him to take her place. LeRoy, our only high school senior, was a young man who rarely said anything in public settings, especially where people outside his age group were present. He lived to ride rodeo, and was looking forward to joining the Miles Community College rodeo team next year. So his willingness to lead came as a happy surprise.

The ten of us were crowded at a round table designed to seat six as LeRoy read a few verses of Bible from the Letter of James. He started at the verse about a bit making the horse obey, and ended with the dangers when our tongues aren't controlled. Then he told us about a recent incident when he and some friends were caught with beer.

I saw Corey's jaw drop as soon as LeRoy began, and the look he gave his friend. Corey must have been one of those beer drinkers. Corey's family were nominally Catholic, but he came with LeRoy because he had a crush on Debbie.

"The cops let us off with a warning." LeRoy was telling about their experience. "The deputy said since it was a first offense for all of us. At least it was the first time they caught us. Except for one guy. I won't say his name. He was throwing beers down pretty fast. The rest of us, we was going slow, scared somebody'd see the bonfire and catch us. And sure enough. Anyhow, that one guy, he was pretty drunk, he cussed out the deputy. He ended up with a night in jail. Me and the others was released for our parents to come get us."

He concluded his account by saying, "Today when Jen asked me to take her turn, my Mom helped me find something in the Bible about horses. Cause you guys know I like to ride the saddle broncs. We found that part in James, and I saw what it was really about .... I didn't think I could tell it." He looked around at us, his expression showing his amazement that he had told it. Then he said simply, "Thanks." He would let us ponder the connections to "that part in James" and "what it is really about."

His story prompted immediate reactions. Mostly the kids wanted to know about LeRoy's treatment by parents who must have been really angry. No one seemed to pay attention to Corey's reaction when the story began. And underage drinking didn't seem to be a concern to any. (topic for a future meeting, perhaps?) I think they were weighing which would be worse, a night in jail or facing the music in the middle of the night at home. LeRoy wouldn't say. I wanted to make a big fuss about how proud I was of silent LeRoy. But I also didn't want to embarrass him back into his shell. He'd given his testimony, and would say no more, except to ask me to do the prayer. I did, praying for his friend in bigger trouble, for all their growing and learning, and even for the people at Prairie Manor that we'd be visiting soon. Preparing for that visit was our plan for this night's meeting.

We heard the wind coming in stronger, which made the adults among us feel anxious to complete our activities and get the kids safely home. After we had played a quick game of knots and begun some discussion about visiting folks at the Manor in two weeks, it became clear that the issues about that visit were different for the older and younger youth. So we split into two very small groups. Kevin could stay with the senior highs, mostly observing.

Kevin told me later about the discussion at their end of the room. Debbie, our take-charge sophomore who had been the prime mover to start the youth program, had appointed herself chair. She led their talk about bringing goodies and entertainment to share with the senior citizens, and meeting a goal to be helpful and make everyone comfortable. She even saw in the reasons we took the younger ones to another table that they should act as mentors to help them overcome any squeamishness about relating with the feeble elderly—who might act or smell funny.

Julia and I joined the seventh and eighth graders, Stephanie, Gordon and Todd, to address their trepidations. Julia described her experience when her parents had to place her grandmother in a nursing home like our Prairie Manor. "We all felt so guilty about it, Mom and Dad and the whole family. Grandma was making sure we would feel guilty, too. Said we didn't care about her anymore. Then, it was only a few weeks later, when we were visiting, she was laughing and telling us about all the funny things the old folks do. Then I didn't have to be made to visit, I wanted to. And I learned to ignore the different smell of the place and the odd ways of senile folks. It still had this impersonal feeling for me, though. With the long halls and rooms all alike. But I could just enjoy the people, especially grandma."

With that reality check, I shared with them the joys of listening to the stories. I told the kids about the need of some to tell memories to someone who hasn't heard it all before a million times.

"Do you have grandparents or great-grandparents who do that?" I asked, but got no answer. Julia and I spoke then in more general terms about the aging process, of the feeble elderly, senile dementia, merely senior, and active seniors. I told of visiting our two church-member story-tellers.

Todd asked, "What kind of stories are they telling you?"

I told them, "Mrs. Carter described a place she said was the prettiest farm you ever did see. She told me how to find it and I went out there. Looked an awful lot like North Dakota to me, which is where it is.

Steph then said, "Pastor Wilson's got my mother asking weird questions to the old folks around town. The old ladies tell him about things, and he looks it all up at the library. Now Mom is going crazy trying to find out this stuff, too."

I said, "It's the stories that keep me going back, and visiting often. And there's a story they almost, but never quite tell enough for me to understand it. I guess I have to keep going back until I get it."

The older youth were waiting for us to finish so that we could do our closing circle. Because listening to the worsening storm had us finishing a little early, we had the kids call their parents to tell them we'd deliver everyone home. Corey, a junior with his own car, had brought LeRoy. Corey was disappointed when we refused his offer to take Deb and her twin sister Danielle home. Dani was as shy as her sister was bold. Outside we found the street mostly clear of snow because it was all blown into a two foot drift on the sidewalk in front of the church. The snow was now coming as a blinding storm and the temperature was dropping rapidly. After some coaxing, the Renault started and I delivered my two shivering passengers to their homes.

***

The blizzard blew and blasted through the night. The wind wasn't blowing nearly as hard by morning, but it kept on snowing. After I saw the four foot drift in the driveway behind the car, I turned the kitchen radio on. While we ate our oatmeal breakfast we listened for school closings. The reports told us which bus routes were cancelled and which would be one and two hours late, but schools stayed open. We would learn that in Eastern Montana snow days are for sissies.

I found it too cold to work at my basement desk, so I brought my journal up to the living room where the girls were playing. I still needed to make some notes about the impressive group of young people I was getting to know. I included some thoughts about what might come next with them. They might be more ready to understand and openly question some of the ideas that the breakfast guys were hearing. In fact, it might be helpful to bring Joe Schmidt over as a guest speaker for a meeting. The kids ought to hear his offbeat ideas about the land and its peoples. Well, not offbeat so much as 'outside the box'.

I closed the journal and put it up where it wouldn't become coloring pages. Then I bundled into a coat that had been idle since last winter in Evanston and went out to shovel the drift. The snow was down to just a few flakes, but the wind was picking up again, sending much of what I dumped off the shovel back where the wind apparently wanted it to stay.

That evening Rachel called to say that even though the forecast looked better for tomorrow (Tuesday) she was canceling our singing group for this week.

27

It was a week, those days leading to Halloween, for weather. Our activities and all our talk seemed to be focused first around the unseasonable cold and, later in the week, around the many sudden changes.

I hadn't heard anything from either the Johnson family or Daryl at Berry Funeral Home, so I assumed their plans didn't include me. That was mostly a relief, but the relief came with a hint of self-doubt.

***

On Wednesday it was just cold and windy. Drifts were being moved around by the ground blizzard. Becca and I picked Ruthie up at school and went to the church. Since kindergarten dismissed earlier than others, we would be early for the second session of our mid-week church school program. We pulled up to the curb, and started unbuckling and unloading from our small car. As I got Becca disentangled from her car seat, Ruthie was yelling from the church entrance, "It's locked, daddy." Someone should be setting up by this time, so I figured the cold was making it hard for her little hands on the button latch. I tried the button, then found my key and unlocked, wondering what this meant.

Once inside, we all went into the office where the phone answering machine was flashing for attention. Four calls from earlier that afternoon had the same message, "No church school today. The schools are announcing it for us." We were so dependent on farm women for our leadership that it shouldn't have surprised me. I had to realize that while we may call them farm or ranch wives, they were all farmers and ranchers, too. I should have learned at least that much from Madge.

I listened to all the messages, with their varied but similar reasons why they couldn't come to town and instead called around to cancel. There was a tug at my pants leg with Becca asking, "Is there turch school? Is Vicky coming?" Vicky was the only other three year old, daughter of one the women who had left a message.

"No, Becca," I answered, "there's no church school this time. Vicky and her mom and dad and her brothers are busy at their farm because of the snow."

Then Ruthie asked, "What should we do?"

A good question. I was slow to answer, instead thinking, "Should I take them on home? This might be a good time for me to visit the elderly lady who lived just around the corner from the church building. But if I take Becca and Ruthie home, I won't want to come back. Maybe they could come with me."

Ruthie was giving up on me, "C'mon Becca." And they were heading toward the nursery door.

"Wait a minute," I said. "Let's go visit Mrs. Rainwater. She lives right by the church."

"Rainwater? Is that her name?" Ruthie gave me an incredulous look.

"Yep. It's English."

"What does she look like?" Ruthie seemed to be trying to get a picture in her head of what someone named Rainwater could possibly look like.

By this time Becca was in the nursery scattering toys around the room. Ruthie was curious enough about a woman named Rainwater that she willingly helped us pick up the toys. I made a note to put on the door in case someone didn't get the cancellation message. We zipped and mittened, and walked to Mrs. Rainwater's house.

***

Everyone addressed her by her last name. I had noted her first name in the church directory, but didn't bother to remember it. She did not hold to the Harstad first naming custom. If she chose to call me Reverend Wilson, I wouldn't suggest anything different.

Mrs. Rainwater welcomed us like long lost kin—who somehow use last names. The house was quite warm, with that musty feel of old furniture and rugs that hadn't been moved in years. In the warmth Ruthie kicked off her boots and peeled off her heavy coat, so Becca did the same, climbing out of her orange snow suit. Mrs. Rainwater admired Ruthie's pretty dress. Ruthie had insisted that she must wear a dress on church school day, in spite of the cold. Her mother insisted on two layers of tights with it.

Becca pointed out her "orange," before Mrs. Rainwater had a chance to direct her admiration to her. Becca had matched an orange t-shirt with her snow suit, a color just different enough to clash. Ruthie was all ready to point this out until Becca gave her a "don't you dare say anything" look.

Mrs. Rainwater led us to the kitchen, with its low work counters piled with the items she needed to reach frequently. She was very small, and made shorter still by a significant osteoporosis hump. As soon as she entered the kitchen she pulled an apron from a hook on the door and tied it on over her flower print housedress. She had me pull the small table away from the wall so that the four of us could sit around it. Coffee was a frequent item to keep within reach, served from a nearly new drip coffee maker on the counter. While she heated water in a small sauce pan, she had me reach the extra mugs and cocoa mix up in the cupboard.

While the kids started on the cookies that Mrs. Rainwater set out on a plate and as she busied herself with the coffee and cocoa preparations, she also started telling about the way it used to be.

"Life was so different when I was their age. Look at us—store bought cookies, hot chocolate from powder and water. When I was a little girl, it would have been warm raw cream, with a little coffee in it if father had bought enough for the winter when he sold the grain that fall. We always had a milk cow, though. This was out on the South Jabbok, before Harstad was even a town. Father had to take the wheat in an enormous wagon down to the railroad along the Yellowstone. He'd be gone for a week with every load. But there weren't that many loads. Mother would worry so when he was gone. We'd think of him sleeping on the ground under that wagon, with the wolves howling."

She could see that this was frightening the girls. What she said next didn't really help, but with it their attention was starting to wane. Before I could stop her, she had refilled the cookie plate. I took two, just to deprive Becca of them.

"It was just us and the animals out there. The roads father took to get to the railway are still wagon tracks, or nearly. There's still no pavement, I don't believe. Still, I'm so glad to have grown up in those times, not like the world the children are facing today."

"Oh, it is different. I don't know if it is worse or better, but it is different," I said.

"It is worse, Reverend Wilson. All the drugs and loose morals today. I can hardly stand to watch TV for what they show now," she asserted, and abruptly returned to her early experiences. "It was so hard for Mother way out there. She came from England. Father came to America first. He worked for a cattle company on the open range. Then, instead of going back to England with the money he saved to win his bride, he homesteaded and also bought to make that fine spread. Mother told me how it was. When he sent for her to come he wrote about his big holdings, his many acres in Montana. She thought she was coming to be the baroness of a royal estate, with servants to order around. She was not prepared for the untamed West. Oh, it was a different life. I'm so glad you brought your lovely young ladies to see me, Reverend Wilson. Seeing the little ones does take me back. I was an only child, the only child for miles. As I grew a little older they would have me stay at a neighbor ranch four or five miles away. They were a big family that lived near the school house. That was the only way to go to school. Father would come for me most Fridays, then take me back on Sunday. Mother would spend days on end hardly leaving her bedroom. She was refined, and never adapted to ranch life. But what else could they do?" The question was rhetorical. The next I would answer. "Have you ever been out that way? Up Jabbok to little South Jabbok Creek?"

"Well, we did drive out the Jabbok Road for a way in the summer. Mostly we noticed how bad the drought had stunted the wheat crop out there," I said.

"Then you have an idea how far you can go without seeing a house or a single person, I expect."

"I saw cattle, though. And antelope, a few deer. You're right—not much evidence of people out there. Hey," I said, "I have a question, Mrs. Rainwater. Have you ever heard of the Nonpartisan League?"

"I have," she said, and stopped. I waited. Then, as she lifted herself to stand by holding onto the table, she said, "Well, this has been a pleasure. I hope you'll come back again soon."

With her dismissal, we climbed back into our warm coats and snowsuit, said our goodbyes and walked back to the car parked in front of the church.

***

It was still too cold for October when we hunkered under our blankets on Thursday night. By the time we got up on Friday a stiff Chinook wind from the southwest was causing the snow to disappear faster than it had arrived.

28

I expected to find a happy Friday breakfast crew at the Hilltop. Instead I found three complainers: Sherm, Cal and Ed. Earlier in the week, although I actually had very little contact with anyone outside my family, I'd heard complaints about having to break into winter feed supplies early—'if this keeps up, what then' complaints—and grumbling about the difficulties getting anywhere as drifts kept piling up and moving. Ed said he tried his snowmobile, but it would just start and die. Now, with the Chinook wind, these few guys who came were complaining about the way all the snow's blessed moisture was being sucked back into the atmosphere and blown away. They even complained about their efforts all week against the drifts, that were now going anyway on their own. "Why did we bother?"

My own complaints of the week were blowing away with the snow. My kids could play outside for more than thirty seconds. I could walk around town without snowshoes—something I didn't even have, of course.

I had taken advantage of days when I could pretend I was snowbound at home. That meant I had an All Saints Day plan for Sunday ready ahead of time. The sermon was a manuscript fully written out on a yellow legal pad. The mimeograph stencil was typed, ready to crank out bulletins on the old Gestetner. And today the church office would warm up quickly for the mimeo ink to flow. I really didn't want any help from my group that might require re-writing.

The eggs and bacon seemed to help the mood around the table begin to lift. The venting of complaints was done and the nourishment eased the exhaustion of the storm days—probably the real reason for our whiny attitudes. Now we were all disappointed that we'd fallen into a bitching session, so we were ready to quit early. How could we have forgotten that Montanans don't complain about bitter weather? We brag about it.

To get us away from weather talk, but still avoid the Bible study we ostensibly gathered for, I talked a little bit about the children's and my visit with Mrs. Rainwater.

All of us joined with Cal in pushing our chairs back as he stood and announced that he was going to be on time for work without having to rush.

Sherm stood, then suddenly snapped his fingers and sat down again. With a gesture he had me pull my chair closer, and said, "I just had a crazy thought, Wil. You ought to get a real sense of how this country is. Joe will back me up, here. You should take my outfit again, and drive up the Jabbok a little, but mostly go down and follow those back roads all the way to the Yellowstone River. You'll see some sights, let me tell you. Do it now. The Chinook makes this the time to go."

"Well, I like your idea, Sherm," I said. "I have some plans for today, though. And I'd like to take the family along this time, but the kids are all excited for Halloween tomorrow, and then it'll probably be winter again, I suppose."

"No, it won't," he replied. "Sunday afternoon will give you plenty of time. Unless you can't allow yourself to let what's-their-names do the youth group without you."

"Their name is Kevin and Julia Lahti. You should get acquainted. They have some good ideas that the church ought to hear about. Anyway, the group doesn't meet this week."

"Humph, newcomers with good ideas. Where have I heard that before." Sherm said this as a statement, not a question. "But no meetings to hold you back, so there you go. Take the truck after church. Tie the little squirts in the jump seats, and go. I'll even leave a good map in the truck for you."

"We'll do it. Thanks," I said. And then I'll tell you all about it and it will inspire Joseph to give us another dissertation on the land. See you Sunday."

Ed had been silent since the complaining time before our food had arrived. Now he left us with a nod and a wave.

"Now I need to get to work, too," Sherm said. By the end of the day I'll have a shop full of Ski-Doos that would've run fine if people would just do the spring shut down the way I taught them to." One of them would be Ed's.

29

I had told Sherm I had plans for the day. To make that true I had to figure out what they were. Plans for Friday: update journal, play with kids, visit Madge—it had been about ten days and I still wanted the rest of the story.

After lunch, Ruthie skipped off to kindergarten and Becca eventually got down to her "but you must" nap. Berta would use that time to put the finishing touches on the Halloween costumes she was making. I put on a light jacket and took a walk through the puddles to Prairie Manor. By then the day was warm enough that even the jacket was hardly needed. I worried that my timing may be wrong. It might be siesta time at the Manor.

When I arrived, residents were mostly on the move, from the dining area to rooms for the afternoon rest, or to the chairs they preferred for watching and dozing. I found Madge alone, still at a dining table with a dinner plate of uneaten mashed potatoes, hamburger and gravy in front of her. To call it Salisbury steak would be to insult both beef loin and the Salisbury plain. Still, it was troublesome that she hadn't eaten. Madge didn't eat much, as a rule, but she did enjoy her meals.

Madge's eyes were open, but she looked like she might be asleep anyway. Her head bowed, staring at her hands folded in her lap. I took a seat opposite Madge at the square table. "Hello Madge," I said, "Pastor Wil from the church."

She looked up but the blank stare continued, and said with little more than a whisper, "Oh, hello Pastor. Did you come to tell me to eat, too?"

"No, but it does concern me. Are you feeling ill or down somehow?"

"Well, I don't know. I'm not hurting, not any more than I always do. I just can't work up any interest for it. Food just doesn't taste good lately."

"But if you don't eat, then nothing will be good, will it."

"Why should that matter? Are you the doctor? Oh, wait a minute. You're the pastor, aren't you." She was starting to perk up just a little, and reached for her spoon.

"Yes, that's right, I'm Pastor Wil.

Madge took a spoonful of potato, swallowed with a sound that made we think she might be choking. But then she said, "That gravy is cold. Who could eat that? Did Buddy get back?"

"Oh, has Buddy been here visiting? Doesn't he live in Rapid City?"

Madge gave me a puzzled look. Then she nodded her head and said, "Oh my goodness, Pastor. I must be dreaming. It must be the blizzard doing it to me. Or else, it's just because....I'm the oldest, you know. Bertram went out in the storm to break bales for the stock—the horses and the milk cow. That was the first big storm in the winter after Elwin was killed. And Buddy didn't have Elwin's trick ready. Elwin would keep a long stretch of clothesline cord coiled beside the door. He'd tie one end to the door handle or a post out there, and the other end he'd tie to his overall. Then if the storm got worse all of a sudden, if the snow blinded him and he couldn't see the house he'd pull the rope and follow it back. This time Buddy went out and the blizzard was blowing hard. After long enough for the chores, I was fretting so. It was all I could do to keep

Ralph from going out to look, and I'd have both of my young men to fret over, and maybe lose. The coil of clothesline was at the barn, don't you know. Well, it was an hour or more when he finally came dragging in, frostbite on the tip of his nose, but otherwise just cold. Said he couldn't see the house, and started in what he thought was the right way, but must've wandered in circles. When the storm let up just enough, he told us, he was another fifty yards in the exact wrong direction. Then it still took time. He saw the house, headed back toward us, and then the wind would gust and he says he just waited then, so he wouldn't go wrong again. And came as fast as he could through the drifts whenever he could see the house, even a little."

"Wow, that must have been a frightening time for all of you," I said.

"We were learning that Pop had good ideas how to survive out there. Maybe he couldn't survive the mob, but he could outsmart the Dakota prairie at its worst. And now we'd have to outsmart it without him. If only we could outsmart the bankers." Madge closed her eyes, then, and her head dropped forward. I reached across for her plate. Her nose was about to land in her dinner when she jerked back to wakefulness.

"Can I walk you to your room for a rest, Madge?" I asked.

"No. I'd rather sit in the big chair over there." She pointed toward the chair where I often found her. I pushed the wheelchair (that she was relying on more and more) across the room, and clumsily helped her maneuver from one chair to the other.

Once we were seated again, I said, "Madge, the last time we visited, you were telling me about how it was back then, when the League was facing more conflict and Elwin was getting more involved, and you wondered, 'How will it end?' And I left you saying I'd be asking you, 'How did it end? Now you tell me that it was a mob. Is that right? Was it a mob that killed your husband?"

"Where will it end? Is that truly what I said? It never really does end, though, does it. It was such a fine party. We heard about a big old picnic and barn dance they were putting on at the Lintner Ranch. It was come one come all. That's the way we did in those days. Elwin was hearing that the League was gaining interest in Montana. So we all came over to Montana, to the Lintner place, for some celebrating. ... And so Elwin could find some sympathetic folks to help organize over here. My but it started out a wonderful party. We danced. The mamas, and the grandmas too, took turns seeing to the little ones, so everybody could have a good time. You know, Pastor Tim..." She said that name, then looked at me, and I clearly was not Tim, my predecessor, so she started again. "You know Pastor, there was one young woman there. A tall girl. She was with her father and mother, had a baby girl. We hardly talked, but I learned her husband was overseas in the war. I saw her being invited to dance, and she'd shake her head, and just watch. Looking lonesome as can be, but she seemed contented just to listen to the music. And, along with her mother, she'd see to the little child. You know who that memory reminds me of? It come to me just now. It's Nilda, somehow Nilda reminds me of that girl so long ago.

"Anyway, we all had a grand time," she continued. 'Elwin would talk to whoever of those farmers he could get to listen. They'd be out in the barnyard or out in the field where the wagons and automobiles were left. But then there was the fight."

Madge paused, tears welled in her eyes. She tried to blame her old eyes, and called out to an aide who was wiping the dining tables, "Could you get me some eye drops, please miss? These old eyes get so tired."

The young aide answered, "In a minute, Madge." But she picked up her rag and disinfectant spray bottle and took the message to an LPN at the desk. Soon she was treated with her drops, which of course were for her dry eyes, not for the times the tear ducts worked better than usual.

"Oh, that night." Madge returned to her remembrance. "How will it end? When word came from the parking field about the fight, the Montana women were all tsk-tsk. Those Fenton boys, they said, always drink too much. They get drunk and try to pick a fight. And if no one will fight them, they fight each other. That's what I was hearing from the women. Tsk-tsk, too proper to go out the door, but wishing they could see a fight all the same. Those were the same women that earlier were talking behind my back about outside agitators from Dakota, just like those IWW communists up in Butte and how the Communist Party was taking over in Plentywood up by the Canada border.

"But about the fight. A man, I think it was Mr. Lintner, the one whose place we were on, whispered in the ear of the man calling the dances. He stopped the band. It was a fine band, too. Everybody from all around the countryside, anyone who played a guitar or fiddle joined in. There was even a tall, skinny boy, maybe 14 or 15 years old who was playing on a big bull fiddle, playing as dandy as can be. Oh, it was a fine party up to that moment. The caller stopped the music and asked for help. George got whacked on the head by a big rock, he said. Didn't say how. He didn't say his brother pushed him and he tripped and fell on a rock in the ground. No, just, 'he got whacked.' But the word among the women was that it was all in the Fenton family as per usual."

Madge daubed her eyes with a tissue and closed them again for a moment before she went on. "George Fenton got hurt. He got whacked. It wasn't a party anymore. That's when it would turn ugly." She became quiet again, controlling the tears that could easily become sobbing.

I wanted to ask again, "How did it end?" but I'm not that stupid.

Just then the nurse returned to our corner. Janet, according to her name tag, said, "I'm sorry to interrupt, but Madge, I'm told you didn't eat any of your dinner today. Doctor will be over later, should I have her check on you?"

Madge said, "No. I'm sure I'll be ready for some supper. Talking to our new pastor here. Worked up my appetite again. Have you two met? Pastor..."

I filled in, "Wil Wilson, good to meet you Janet."

She replied, "Good to meet you, Pastor. Janet Schmidt."

"Schmidt, huh," I said. "Are you related to Joseph?"

"You know Crazy Uncle Joe?"

"Yes, I really like him."

"Oh, me too. I love him to death. He's my husband's uncle. We call him crazy 'cause of his big ideas. He'll bend your ear for hours if you let him."

"Yeah. That's why I like him. We just met a few weeks ago, so I haven't had an overload of his philosophizing yet."

Madge had been trying to get Janet's attention. "I need to go to my room now, Miss." A new odor told us she meant it. "Good bye, Pastor Wil. Thank you for coming." She remembered my name, and I realized that today's earlier forgetfulness was actually something new.

"I'll come again soon. Blessings on you, Madge."

A fight. Then it gets ugly. How did it end? I was sure that I would come again very soon. I was getting more concerned about Madge's declining health. For her, yes, but she had lived long. She's the oldest, you know. My desire was to hear how it ends. I was convinced that she needed to tell it, too. For her whole life story to end well, this story needed to be told.

30

By Saturday, Halloween, we all were growing weary of the adage, but still said it. Within the first minute or so every conversation included the line: "If you don't like the weather in Montana, just wait a minute." Except the kids. They had another phrase of the day: "Trick or treat." They practiced all day. In mid-afternoon Dani Becker called, offering to take our girls trick-or-treating around the neighborhood. Berta wasn't so sure she could give up that role, but when she heard Dani's reason for offering, she said yes. And figured they both might go out with the little girls.

Dani arrived a little before dusk, just as arranged. She was outfitted as Indiana Jones, with the right kind of hat, mascara whiskers, and whip. Dani was dealing with her feelings at being left out. Her twin sister Deb was going with Corey to a costume party at McCracken's enormous house. If Deb were without a date, the both would have gone. All of a sudden going dateless was uncomfortable. So much so that she had even withstood Deb's insistence that she come along with them. So, we welcomed her help and tried to make it as fun as we could, knowing it could never be fun enough.

It was still amazingly warm as Princess Leia and the clown left with Berta and Dani following. The oversized clown suit bulged and blew in the warm breeze. Leia's white gown had the extra cloth gathered with a gold Christmas garland. Berta had made the outfits during the blizzard. She expected them to be worn over snow suits. Tonight, even though the wind grew cooler as the sun went down, a sweater was all the kids needed.

I stayed home, answered the door, and worried that we might not have enough candy. I really hoped to save some chocolate for myself. Berta, Dani, Ruthie, and Becca all returned together after about an hour, buckets loaded with goodies. Becca, overtired and fussy, was demanding to be taken out for more. Within minutes, sitting on the sofa, while examining with her extortion haul, she tipped sideways, sound asleep. If they had been together the whole time, I wondered, why did the conversation between Berta and Dani seem to be just beginning? Berta explained later that she had only gone with them as far as next door, and spent the hour with Mary Ann on their big front porch greeting the little monsters and witches.

Taking an outing away from the candy overload the next day looked as if it could be a good plan.

***

Nilda was in her usual pew on All Saints' Day, but this was the third week in a row that Madge had been absent. In our silent prayer time, her tired face appeared in my mind's eye, growing weaker even as I prayed for her.

Just as soon as the church service ended Berta drove the girls home to have lunch and get ready for our drive through the back country. As Sherm and I did the traditional handshake at the door, he said, "Let's grab a quick cup of coffee downstairs, and you can run me home in the truck. Karl can close up here."

"Sounds good to me," I said. "The kids are excited about our little adventure. I hope we don't disappoint them."

To our quick cup of coffee we added a big chunk of Frieda's famous cherry-chocolate cake. Frieda overheard Sherm telling Karl why he would have the honor of being the last out and locking the doors. So she sent me out with a plate wrapped in foil, saying as she handed it to me, "Here's some cake for Berta and the little ones. You've had your chocolate, so I put a slice of the apricot kuchen in for you."

Sherm grabbed me before I could let myself get pulled into more conversation. With a thank you wave we headed up the stairs. Once outside, he tossed me the keys and I drove him home in his vehicle. I only saw him wince once, when I upshifted to third too soon.

"I saw that, Sherm," I said. "I'll be more careful about the gear changes."

"You're doing fine, Wil," he replied. "Just be real careful you don't let a washout surprise you out there."

Ruthie handed me a peanut butter sandwich as I walked in the door at home. "I made this for you, daddy." It had a child's tender loving squishiness about it. That enhanced the flavor so that I ate it in about five bites. I changed into jeans and sweatshirt, loaded the box of snacks and drinks, to which I added the cake package, and we were ready to explore north down Jabbok Creek. The afternoon was warm, too warm for November, but Berta took no chances. Warm coats and hats were added to our load. The truck cab that had seemed so huge the other time, was now packed with family—accessorized.

Kids buckled into jump seats in the narrow extended cab area, we headed toward the westbound highway. Becca, noticing the aluminum foil package on top of the snacks and sodas in the box between her and her sister, asked, "What's that?"

I answered, without even trying to see what she was asking about, "That's for later, Becca."

She persisted in asking, so I ignored her. Her mother could answer honestly, "I don't know."

I had driven this stretch of highway several times since our move to Harstad, but hadn't paid careful attention to the side roads along the way. After about a half hour at highway speed, we came to the Jabbok Road turn off. I had taken it south during a summer exploration and ranch visit. I expected to find a junction, with the road going north as well. So, we pulled off the road for a closer look at the map Sherm had provided. What had looked like a junction had a little jog at the highway. During the stop we made the girls stay in the awkward jump seats, in spite of the whining, with a promise of "pretty soon."

Within a half mile we found the road going north, really northwest. The compass Sherm had recently mounted on the dashboard was a nice addition. Sherm's map said Jabbok. The sign, that we wouldn't have noticed cruising the highway, called this Hoffman Road. Did we miss something? It was a narrow, rough road, but we determined to try it anyway. About three miles further, the narrow road ended at a better graded scoria road going straight north and south. Maybe we turned too soon. After another half hour of slow travel, we came into hill country. The road followed along the little stream, then up over hills, and down into cottonwood groves. The road was clear, but there were still many snowdrifts in the barrow pits on each side.

When Becca asked, "Is it later now?" we stopped at a stand of cottonwoods for some run around time—and cake. We must have been in the middle of a huge ranch. There wasn't a fence line in sight. I tried to explain to my little girls that we were traveling the route Mrs. Rainwater's father took long ago, with a wagon, pulled by horses or oxen, to sell his wheat. They were happy to tell their mother about Mrs. Rainwater, but weren't really interested in the reason for our outing.

We walked together down along the small creek with the grownups trying to avoid the drifts and children climbing them. It was there, in an open area beside the stream, that we found something unexpected.

***

It was Ruthie who saw it first. "Why are those stones like that, Daddy?"

"Which stones?" was my reply.

"These ones. They're in a circle." And she spun in a circle pointing around her.

Berta said, "Wow! That's a tepee ring, Ruthie. Look, there's another over there." She pointed about ten yards further along the creek.

"What's a tepee ring?" the girls chorused.

"Well, you know what a tepee is, right?" Berta asked.

Ruthie explained, "A tepee's a kind of house. We learned about different kind of houses in school. I like the yurt."

"What's a yurt?" asked Becca.

"Let's think about the house that those stones tell us about, okay?" Berta said.

Pointing to an old, fallen cottonwood, I said, "How about we sit over there on that big log for a minute."

We sat, Ruthie on my lap, Becca on Berta's.

"What do you know about tepees, Ruthie?" I asked.

"That's a house where Indians live. And they take it with them and put it up and take it down like a tent when we go camping. But I don't know what the stones are for."

"The stones were used to hold the sides of the tepee down so the wind didn't blow in. In the old days they were made with buffalo hides," Berta answered.

Then I said, "Not too many people live in tepees anymore."

"Alvin does," Ruthie said loudly. "His grampa and gramma and his whole family live in a tepee at Crow Fair. He told us. Teacher said to bring a picture, but he didn't."

"Really, Alvin lives in one every summer for Crow Fair. Cool," I said. "Do I know Alvin?"

Berta said, "He's a classmate of Ruthie's, Alvin Bird."

"I guess I live in my little Community Church circle. I thought everyone in Harstad claimed either German or Norwegian heritage," I said.

"There are probably as many Irish, you know," Berta said. "But speaking of tepee rings—these stones tell us that some families stayed here sometime. They either camped for a short time following the animals that they hunted. Or, maybe this was even a place to spend the winter. Look around. There aren't any snow drifts in here. There's wood to make fires for cooking and warmth, and to melt ice for drinking water if they had to. The deer would come to the creek to drink nearby."

Berta pointed to a dense thicket on the other side of the creek. "Oh, look at those bushes. There's no leaves or berries at this time of year, so I can't tell what kind of plant, but I suspect there are edible berries there sometimes. This might have been a place for harvesting fruit, maybe more than hunting."

"People lived around here, traveling to wherever the best hunting and gathering food from plants would take them," I said. "My friend Mr. Schmidt thinks that the land where we live will turn us back into nomads. Nomad means people who don't live in just one place, they move from place to place."

"We moved. Are we nomads?" Becca asked. She'd been feeling left out. Her big sister seemed to know so much.

"In a way, I guess we are, Becca. The house we live in isn't ours—it's there for the person who comes to be pastor at the church. And it seems like they change every three or four years at Harstad. I hope we don't have to be nomads again that soon." I was drifting off into my own dream state, away from our little learning opportunity.

Berta brought us back. "Let's look around a little more here. Where there's a tepee ring, there might be other treasures from the people who camped here." We started to get up. Berta stopped us for another moment. "But wait. Don't pick anything up. Just show us what you find. Where we are doesn't belong to us, and we don't want to interfere with archaeology."

I waited for the question 'what's archaeology?' It didn't come. Instead, as the girls jumped down from our laps, the word was, "We won't touch anything. We'll just point."

And they mostly kept their word. But a half-buried arrowhead was worth examining. Then we put it back. If I had only remembered to bring the camera, I could have photographed it to learn more about the era, maybe the tribe, and of the encampment from someone who knows about these things.

We had set out to learn about the difficulty of hauling grain to the rail head. Our trip had given me some clues about that. But our trip took us further back in time, and reminded me about the human displacement that took place for this to become a wheat hauling trail. Is Joe right? White settlement was only eighty years old, and the settler population was much smaller than it had been sixty years earlier. Harstad was no longer kept alive by the agriculture, but now by the oil patch. And that will one day disappear, too.

We knew how long it would take to get home if we retraced our route. We did not know how far we still were from the Yellowstone River. We'd had a wonderful outing, so we went back the way we came. As we drove, I thought of Madge and her family, traveling these dirt tracks from North Dakota for a party. I thought of Elwin, and a chance to sell a big idea, of farmers taking control of their economy with a Nonpartisan League. And I remembered her words at our last visit. "Then things got ugly."

31

Fall weather with gusty wind returned on Monday. Sherm seemed unconcerned that I didn't return his truck until afternoon. I needed the sweater and jacket I was wearing for the walk from the machine shop to Prairie Manor. I hoped to visit both Nilda and Madge on a day without other obligations. I had my steno pad in hand. Nilda wouldn't want me to take notes, and I usually got so engrossed in Madge's remembrances that I forgot to write. But I was ready.

As I walked I pondered what I might learn today. Nilda had been telling the struggles of her father and husband, of conditions that reminded me of the traumatic stress problems of a couple friends who had fought in Viet Nam. She might just be able to tell me more about the events that caused her father to change.

Madge might be able to tell enough about the barn dance to get through the 'ugly', and maybe experience some release. I prayed that she would be feeling better, eating better, more herself today.

Nilda met me just inside the door, cane at the ready if I should try to ignore her. Did she think it was Tuesday? Surely she didn't expect to see me on a Monday. We walked to her room, got seated, and looked out at a gray sky and an empty park playground. Nilda was ready to talk, so I got ready to listen. She gave a skeptical glance at my steno notebook, so I set it aside on the foot of her bed, and took off my jacket. The sweater kept me too warm in this building that was always kept at the comfort levels of the elderly.

***

"Pastor Wil, I do thank you for putting up with me. Since you let me lean on you so much. I'm starting to feel better, at least I think so. You don't get after me for being such a grump, not like some of the staff here. They won't even give me the time of day. But you, Pastor, you just accept it and then we give it all to God."

"Well, Nilda, I'm glad to help as best I can. You can always lean on the Lord. Now, don't take this wrong, but did you hear yourself just now?"

"What?"

"Nilda, when you said, 'they don't give me the time of day'?"

"Oh! I was still being a complaining grump, wasn't I."

"I'm glad you're willing to see it," I said. "And you really aren't so much a grump, are you?" (I did not say, 'not like the guys before breakfast last week,' but I thought it.) "You know that the staff are overworked and underpaid. They have to see to needs of everyone here, so they just can't give any one person the time and attention they really need. And besides, you are less dependent on the aides than most."

"Why I bring it up, Pastor, is that I was remembering again," Nilda said. "I got to wondering when I changed from the happy child into what I've been for so many years. And I believe it started while Walter was in the war. I was back staying with Mom & Papa. My brother John was still there, too, running the ranch with Papa. John was a cattleman while Papa stayed in charge of the crop farming. Herbert went off to work in Fargo at that time—expecting to get drafted, but he didn't. He came back to the ranch a few years later."

Nilda paused, then got back to her story, saying, "It was when Magda was a baby, about four months old, and it was getting close to my first wedding anniversary. There I was, with a baby who hadn't met her daddy. My husband was on the other side of the world in the trenches in France, with nothing but a grainy picture of his daughter. I got so down in the dumps and I just couldn't climb out. Mom and Papa tried everything they could to cheer me up.

"That's when they decided we should all go to the barn dance at the Lintner's. We always helped at their branding time. All the neighbors helped each other, taking turns at branding the calves. They still do. But we were joined up with the German church by then. We didn't dance or play cards. Sure, they let me and my brothers do Christian Endeavor with the Lintner girls, but Papa never knew about what we listened to on the Victrola after our meetings. But that year, summer of '18, Mom and Papa were so desperate to see me happy that we went to the big barn party. And look where that got us. Oh my stars, look where that got us."

This time the pause seemed very long. I waited, expecting to hear where that got us, but it didn't come. Finally I tried some reflecting, "You got low enough that your parents were ready to try anything, even going against church rules. Did the barn dance help?"

The pause continued as Nilda looked around and gave indications that she was about to speak several times before she finally found her voice. "Did the dance help? That night it did. And I had forgot that it did. It wasn't the dance that brought more trouble. That night it did help. There were other young mothers there with babies and little ones. Women that I always saw before as the grown-ups. Now I was one of them, too. They were real helpful, just by how they took care of their youngsters with such confidence and ease. I was kind of resentful about Mom always telling me how to take care of Magda. Now I look back and think if she wouldn't have been there to see to the baby, and see that I saw to my baby, what if, umm, what horrible things might've happened in my melancholy.

"Now you call it depression. Then the doctors called it melancholy. The midwife spotted it one time when she came to see how Magda was getting along. Wish I could remember her name, that midwife was such a help. She took charge, she did. Put me and Magda in her Ford car and drove us into Harstad to see Dr. Schneider. See, I remember his name. But he was around for years and years. The midwife must have left the country when so many farms went bust in the dry. I've seen dry, worse even than this summer and without these nice fall rains.

"And dry I was, a drought inside of me. Dr. Schneider said melancholy. But didn't have any real help. Now we got pills for everything. Then it was just buck up and get on with doing what I needed to do every day. I plodded on. And then we all went to the Lintner's party. You know who one of the young mamas I met at that party was? Can you guess?" Nilda brightened as she asked her quiz question.

"Well, how would I know that?" I said. "Wouldn't be Madge, would it?"

"Why Pastor Wil," she chirped, "got it in one!" "She was one of those calm mothers dealing with the squabbles among the children with such control. She'd be watching the kiddies and at the same time proudly watching her husband doing his political wheedling among the farmers. That's the only time I met her back then. They came over from Dakota. I think it was the opportunity to promote his Nonpartisan League into Montana they came for, and nothing more. Unless he really was a Communist Wobbly. Look where that got us."

The statement brought a long pause, just as those words had before. This time I just waited, sensing the tension until I was feeling very tense as well.

Finally, Nilda said, as she fought back tears, "Can we just have our prayer now? I thought I could tell you, but not today, I guess."

We prayed about the effort and difficulty and to be open to grace in the telling that would come. I departed, feeling tense and frustrated. So, I prayed into the silence as I walked down the hall and out the door. A visit with Madge would have to wait until another day. Writing the thoughts in my journal that night brought the frustration back and led to a fitful night's sleep, wondering, 'Has Nilda ever really recovered from her melancholy?'

32

I wasn't ready to stay at Prairie Manor and visit with Madge immediately after Monday's meeting with Nilda. Now it was Tuesday and I could hardly restrain myself from running to the Manor hours before our singing time. The journal writing process of Monday evening included some review of earlier entries, bringing questions and concerns to the surface. One lingering question was: How does the fight and whatever happened next relate to the Nonpartisan League? It's always there in the background, but how does it connect? After lunch, I pulled out my interlibrary loan book, *Political Prairie Fire*. Maybe I'll see something about the way the League operated that will help me ask the right questions.

Before I could open the book, the writing on a paper band around the cover introduced a different anxiety. The book was due last Friday. Interlibrary could cost a little more than my typical late return. I was off to the library. As the library door banged loudly behind me, Sophie looked up from her work at the front desk and called out, "Hello Wil, I was just about to call you. You're a little late."

I replied, "Quiet! This is a library." I put the overdue book on the counter and asked, "How much is this going to cost me?"

Sophie answered with a grin, "How much have you got?"

"That bad, huh." I reached for my wallet.

"No, Rev. How does sixty cents sound?"

Relieved, I handed her a dollar, pocketed the change, and started to turn around.

"Just a minute, Wil," Sophie said. "I have some information that will interest you. Come and sit for a bit."

We sat at a table where she could keep an eye on the entrance. We seemed to be the only people among the books this early afternoon. "I've been learning a lot recently. So much that I'm really anxious to talk with Madge again," I said.

"Well, what I have to tell you might just surprise you with something unexpected. You might even find some real leads about the killing, or at least particulars to ask Madge about. I managed to get one of my reluctant oldsters to really open up and tell me something."

She paused. I said, "And?"

"This guy's a real geezer: tall, skinny guy with hollow cheeks and stringy white hair. He comes in a couple times a week, always pulls his big hat off as he walks through the door. He wears these boots made for stirrups and not for walking. The guy has this permanent look as if he just rode in from two months on the open range.

"Anyway," she continued, "he comes in to read the newspapers, and such. I've asked him some questions to get him talking about the old days. He has some great stories, but until just recently he wouldn't answer any of my questions about the Nonpartisan League. Or anything political, for that matter. But one day, I think it was when the snow was on its way and it was getting colder, the library was empty like today, and he was ready to sit and talk for a while. He told me how he used to play the bull fiddle for all the country dances and parties. He started as a kid, because his uncle had the stand-up bass and let him teach himself to play. So he got to reminiscing about playing in the band, and told about a time, at a big ranch party when he was about fifteen or sixteen, when a Wobbly agitator was stirring up trouble. That's what he called him: a Wobbly agitator from North Dakota."

"Hmm, I know the IWW was active up in Butte at one time. Was it really the Industrial Workers of the World operating over here and in North Dakota?" I wondered aloud.

"I think the man got it a bit wrong on that score," Sophie said. "I have a feeling, from some other things he said, that the Wobbly was really a Nonpartisan League organizer."

"Is there any chance we're talking about a party at the Lintner Ranch?" I asked.

"He didn't say where it was." Sophie edged forward, looked me in the eye and asked, "Hey, do you already know something about this?"

"I think maybe so," I said, "but go on."

She went on. "He said there was a fight outside. He didn't see it because he was playing in the band inside the barn. But he said that the Wobbly bashed his friend George's head with a rock and hurt him badly. And, before long—I don't know if that meant hours or days—before long, the problem was taken care of, he told me, and no more Wobbly traitors would stir things up in Kirchen County any more."

"Did you ask him what he meant by "taken care of"?

"I asked what happened to the Wobbly. It was pretty clear, even though he wouldn't give me a direct answer. He said the problem was taken care of and that there never was a trial about the attack on George."

"Wow," I said, "I'm surprised, but not because this is all new to me. What you've told me fits with a whole lot of stuff I've learned just in the past few days. I was even told that there was a tall, lanky, teenage boy playing the bass fiddle at the Lintner's party. I have heard about a fight, but it isn't clear who was actually involved. It seems George and his brother Sam would always drink and fight at these shindigs. They'd try to pick a fight and if there were no takers, they'd fight each other. I was told that the reality was just that. George fell against a rocky outcropping while he was tussling with Sam. Maybe that was just Madge's cover story that she's come to believe in long years of memory. One thing becomes clear to me. Your Wobbly wasn't from the IWW. He was Elwin Bowdler, unofficial NPL promoter. I have got to talk with Madge before our singing group today."

"And what then?" she said. "When you know how he was killed, what then?"

"I don't know. I do know that I'd also like to talk with the man who told you all this. A geezer, you said. If I'm making the right connections he's not quite eighty years old."

"I'm afraid I can't help you meet him. I don't think he'd like it that I passed his story on to anyone."

I changed the subject to close with a little other business. "But speaking of nursing homes and teenagers, don't forget that youth group is at 3:00 Sunday, not 6, and we're going to visit old folks at the Manor." With that we said goodbye. Sophie went to offer help to a couple of browsers who'd come in, and I to find something to do at my office until it was time to visit Madge (assuming I could get past Nilda's cane of coercion).

33

Nilda was on a settee near the front entry talking with someone when I arrived. She waved with a gesture that could have been a simple greeting, or it might have been urging me along. I returned the wave and said something in greeting and proceeded to the great room to find Madge. And there she was, in her usual seat, head bent forward, eyes closed, mouth open, snoring, but not loudly. I brought a chair from the dining end, sat facing her, and woke her by tapping her on the arm while I said, "Good afternoon, Madge."

"Oh, hello sir." After she pushed her glasses up her nose she started again. "Why, hello Pastor Wil. Good to see you."

"Sorry to wake you."

"That's fine. I was just checking my eyelids for holes. I can do that because," and here she raised her voice to be heard by others nearby, "I'm the oldest you know."

"No you are NOT," came a shouted rebuttal from a couch further along the same wall.

Madge laughed. Then she got serious. "I suppose I have to tell you about it all, don't I. I really did love Elwin, still do. And he wasn't a fighter. That was a big lie to get rid of him. A big lie because they believed a big-big lie. They thought he was something he wasn't. He was just a farmer looking for justice, not some crazy rabble rouser. They turned him into some kind of Joe Hill type. That wasn't my Elwin. My man was a talker, though. He and Mr. Carter were alike that way—both talkers. Maybe that talk was too dangerous after all. But Elwin could talk a man out of hitting him while his fist on the way to his face. So I just don't believe what they said about the fight. I still love him. Will I see him again? Is that your belief?"

I really didn't want to get into particulars of what heaven might be like. I especially would rather avoid the question that Jesus was asked about a woman who'd survived several husbands, 'whose wife will she be?' with Jesus' answer that basically said, 'you don't get it.' So I did say, "I think that what matters is your belief, Madge. I would ask you: How do you see him now? Maybe—think about the time he held your first baby, when Buddy was a newborn. What do you see? Whatever heaven is like you have those memories with you always."

"That's a sweet picture you put in my head. And I thank you for it. But I can't get rid of that other picture. They dumped his dead body like he was no more than a sack of potatoes....right there on the yard between the house and the barn." Madge turned to stare out the window as tears welled up and she began to whimper softly.

She composed herself once again, turned to look at me and said, "My God, but that's an ugly wall out there. Good thing my vision's going."

I said, "I'm sure the children who painted it meant well. But that sure doesn't make it art." When Madge stayed quiet for a long pause I added, "Who were they? Who did that to your husband?"

"Here's the way I see it, Pastor. I told you about the barn dance, didn't I?"

"Yes, you did," I replied. "There was a fight. I think you said it was between two brothers. But after that it got ugly, you said."

Madge squeezed her eyes shut and her fingers twitched for a moment before she spoke. "It was a clear starlit night. Cool and pleasant, with a half-moon giving some light. Elwin came into the barn, gathered us all together, the youngsters and me. He said we have to go home now. Oh, we resisted. We expected to camp in and under our wagon. But we didn't resist for long. We saw the look of fear on Elwin's face, so we gathered up our things and went out. He was already hitching up the horses by the time Buddy and Ralph got there to help. Like I said, the moon was enough to give us some light for travel. Buddy walked in front to guide us and keep us to the road. Plow horses don't move fast, you know.

"Once we were on our way, Elwin told us what happened. He said it was those young Fenton men fighting each other. And there was a bad accident when Sam pushed and George tripped, drunk as he was. He bounced his head off a half-buried rock. But somebody saw a way to turn the accident into something else. I never learned who started it, but once the rumor started it spread like wildfire through those nerve-edgy fellows. They were scared for George, knocked out cold. Somebody—I never did learn who—claimed it was Elwin, they called him the Wobbly agitator, who whacked George with a big rock."

Madge stopped, daubed her eyes with a threadbare white handkerchief that she pulled from her sleeve. Seeing this, I wondered if it would be disruptive to her if I got up and found a box of Kleenex. I took the chance, excused myself saying, "I'll be right back," quickly found tissues, gave her a couple, and put the box on the end table beside her.

She pushed her hanky back in her sleeve and wiped her nose with a tissue. Now she was ready to continue. "Elwin said he wasn't anywhere near the fight. He knew it was no mistake. It was deliberate. To frame him and the Nonpartisan League—both. He said all that time he was talking up the League with a few farmers, some that was worried about being foreclosed. And that's what my Elwin would've been doing. No doubt about it.

"Well, we headed for home in the middle of the night. You ever try to follow a wagon track across country without a headlight or anything? If it wasn't for that half-moon we'd have been lost for sure. We were almost home, but the moonlight helped some others, too. Five men on horseback, claimed to be deputized and Elwin was not going back to Dakota. We were already in North Dakota, nearly to our farm, and they knew it, too. Elwin was shaking like a leaf, but he talked so calm to them. Said they had no jurisdiction. Said he'd be at home if the Sage County sheriff wanted to find him. They were talking there on the road. I think the horsemen, the posse, was just stalling for time because along came a motorcar. The Kirchen County sheriff got out, told Elwin he was under arrest for assault with a deadly weapon and attempted murder. Elwin tried to tell him. 'No,' he said, 'no. I was with some farmers, just talking. Not even near the fight. We just came to help when the man was laying on the ground, out cold. They said he fell.' But the sheriff wouldn't listen. And he didn't care whether he was in Montana or not, said he was in hot pursuit so he had a right to take Elwin to Harstad and let the judge decide."

"And you and your children had to just watch all this," I said. "Buddy and Ralph were at ages where they might have been hard to control. I wonder, ...did they cause any trouble, seeing their father mistreated that way?"

"That's another part I try to forget, Pastor. Buddy did start to reach for the Winchester. We carried a shotgun, mostly in case we ran across a coyote or some other varmint. I saw Buddy make that move. I saw him out of the corner of my eye and gave him such a slap. I hadn't spanked that boy since he was eight, and never with such force has I gave him on the ear that night. I don't like to remember. A mama's not supposed to hit her children. But it was the fear in that moment that made me do it. It was me slapping him that got the posse's attention. All of a sudden three guns was pointed at us. And Buddy just reached his hands out wide, like he was hanging on the cross with Jesus. I'm sorry, Pastor Wil, am I being heretical?"

"More like vividly descriptive, about a very frightening, awful experience." We both sat in silence for a minute or more after I said this. Then I said, "They took Elwin over here to Harstad, did they?"

"The sheriff and the other man who rode with him in the car tied Elwin's wrists and put him in the back seat. Sheriff told one of the other men to follow us and make sure we would get home. I don't think it was really for our protection. I had my strong tribe with me. They didn't want us to follow them, is what I think. Ended up being two of those men rode along behind us, and stayed out by our gate until morning. They kept us prisoners in our own home so we couldn't go back and find out why we heard gunshots before we got all the way home."

As Madge found a couple more tissues to wipe her tears, I realized that I was crying, too. "You actually heard guns fired that night?"

"The sound was far off. Buddy reined the horses and stopped the wagon. But one of those two big-shot posse guards behind us said, 'Just you keep moving. Time to get you on home.'" Madge said this in a low gruff voice, then took our conversation on one of its frequent detours. "You know, it turns out one of those fellows was a banker. Rode horse like a banker, too—sore in the saddle, even going so slow. Mr. Carter had to deal with him for finance at the Mercantile. I wouldn't even go inside the First State Bank of Harstad to deposit a day's receipts with that man there. Mr. Carter had to do that himself. It was the bankers along with the managers for railroads and mills that had it in for the League."

"So you're telling me that the powerful men of the community used a trumped up charge against Elwin to stop the League from growing in this part of Montana." I thought I was asking a question, but it came out as a statement.

"Did they have any idea what they were getting into that night?" Madge's question didn't expect an answer. "I don't expect they planned a murder, but that's what happened. We heard the shots. And the next day all that was left of Elwin was dumped in the yard. There's so much I don't know about what happened in between. Oh, I might've been told, too. Some things we're meant to forget, I believe."

"I think you're right about that, Madge," I said. "Sometimes a memory is best lost to keep us sane. You seem to be at a point now where you want a clear memory. Is that right?

Madge spoke as if I hadn't said anything. "We buried Elwin up on a little rise, away from the house and barn, right there on the farm. There was no money for undertakers. The sheriff at Sage wouldn't give us the time of day. He did not want to get involved in any way. What a lazy, corrupt SOB he was! I wonder, you know, if the Kirchen sheriff was in on the killing, or if he got waylaid by the lynch mob, or what. I've seen dry in this long life I'm living."

"It's just possible, Madge, that I might be able to find some answers. You're not the only one still troubled by your husband's murder. I don't know enough to say more just now, but I'll be asking." Saying that, I looked at my watch. Singers would be arriving soon. To conclude this visit I offered to have some prayer time with Madge. She was ready to let go and let God, at least for now. I would see that we included "Smiles" in our song fest.

34

For the next couple of days I kept to the routines of mid-week church school, appointments and study time. All the while, discoveries from Nilda, Sophie, and Madge crowded my thoughts. Is there more I can know? If so, will that knowledge help Madge? What can it all mean for us now?

On Friday morning I drove to the café with these questions, adding: "What will my co-conspirators at the breakfast table have to say?"

Arriving a little late, I found six men around the six chair table engaged in animated conversation. No one moved to make room for another chair. I set my books on the table between Gary and Joe and tried to edge a chair in. Still no acknowledgement of my presence. Sally brought me a steaming mug of coffee and said as she handed it to me, "Looks like you're getting a fraternity hazing, Pastor Wil. Don't ever be two minutes late."

Gary looked up at Sally, lifted his mug for a refill, but also edged aside. Joe moved a little too, and I squeezed in with my chair.

"Good morning, Pastor," was said by all, but not quite together. "Glad you could make it."

I replied, "Good morning. Don't mind me, go on with what you were talking about."

Cal said, "I think it's time for your Bible lesson now."

"What about Gary's joke," I said.

"Either you missed it, or you didn't get it, Wil. I'm not saying which," Gary said.

"Okay," I said, "the joke is here now. It's been an eventful week of history stories for me. It makes for some questions about what happens now, because of what some people have been carrying on their heads and hearts for decades. But if you want to start with the Gospel for this Sunday, we can do that."

I opened my Revised Standard Bible to Mark 12 and handed it to Ed. I asked him to read verses 38 to 44.

Saying, "I don't have my reading glasses," Ed handed the Bible on to Karl. He started to pass it on to Sherm, but thought better of it and read:

> And in his teaching he said, "Beware of the scribes, who like to go about in long robes, and to have salutations in the marketplaces, and the best seats in the synagogues and places of honor at feasts, who devour widows' houses and for a pretense make long prayers. They will receive the greater condemnation."

> And he sat down opposite the treasury, and watched the multitude putting money into the treasury. Many rich people put in large sums. A poor widow came, and put in two copper coins, which make a penny. And he called his disciples to him, and said to them, "Truly I say to you, this poor widow has put in more than all those who are contributing to the treasury. For they all contributed out of their abundance; but she out of her poverty has put in everything she had, her whole living."

After a long pause, I asked, "Any comment? Is this only about the Jerusalem temple, or does it have a message for us, too?"

"Wil, I remember hearing the story of the widow's mite in Sunday school—before I quit," Joe said. "We all admired the widow's trust and then went out and picked on the fat kid like always. So, here's the deal. I have to think it would say something to us but we probably don't want to hear it."

"Is that right? You guys agree with that?" I asked.

Karl responded, "You know, I think I'd have turned out a lot worse of a person if it weren't for things Jesus tries to tell me. I don't live up to an example like that widow, but it makes me stop and consider. And Frieda makes sure to remind me."

Karl's good friend Ed couldn't help himself. He said, "You could've been even worse than you are?"

"Now boys, let's be nice." This came from young Gary before I could say it.

I did say, "This week when I opened this passage, it was the first part that got my attention. About the big shots in fancy suits, expecting to be treated best, who drone on in long prayers for pretense. Praying to impress people, not to listen for God. Who fits that description in our experience? Is it preachers like me, or what?"

Cal said, "I think you have more you want to say about that. You better go ahead, and I expect it will be interesting. So, of course, we're working twenty miles further out this week and I have to go to work now. I might ask you about it later. I want to hear, if it's about your eventful history week." And Cal was on his way to his pickup by the time we said goodbye.

"Cal set it up for you, Rev," Gary said. "Let's hear it."

"It all came at once. A few days ago I heard an account of the killing in 1918. And also, pieces of the events around it from two other sources. Now we're hearing Jesus go after the powerful elites who act like they deserve it. In the Gospel they seem to be the religious lawyers and leaders, and the academics. But, in our culture, would he say the same thing about the wealthy business leaders and politicians who protect their wealth?"

"What are you getting at, Wil? You're not exactly making yourself clear," came Joe's challenge.

"I'll try, but maybe I'm too confused myself to make it very clear," I said. "Madge struggled through the story she's been trying to tell for a couple months, but it was always too painful to say. She finally blurted out the awful way her husband's body was treated. Then she managed to tell what she saw that night. She didn't see the actual killing, so she still doesn't know just how it happened. But a mob was involved in some way. The people with economic power used a fight to falsely accuse— this is according to Madge, you understand—to accuse Elwin of assault. Last she saw him alive, he was being taken into custody by the Kirchen County Sheriff, even though they were in North Dakota at the time. She's convinced that her husband wasn't involved in the fight at all. But he was recruiting for the Nonpartisan League in Montana that day and evening. And some of the nearly broke farmers were responding to his pitch. Do you think that's anything like the guys in Mark's Gospel, who expect the best seats at dinner and devour widow's houses?"

"They're both a long time ago, Pastor," Karl said. "But yes, there's probably a reason we call the richest people 'filthy' rich." That got a tension relieving chuckle from the group.

"I heard other accounts of the barn dance party that led up to all this," I said. "I got this second hand, but one person who was inside the barn at the time believes that the organizer— that would be Elwin—was a Wobbly, an agitator for the Industrial Workers of the World. This individual holds to the view that a Wobbly assaulted and tried to kill George Fenton. There's this view handed down that Kirchen County took care of a communist threat, a Butte style communist threat at that."

Joe was squirming and gesturing with his fork for attention. "Power corrupts. It sounds to me like it was all about fear. The guys making money off the farmers' troubles were afraid of losing their gold mine. For some poor farmers the worst was already happening, so they had nothing more to fear. And that would make the powers more afraid, wouldn't it. You have to keep the powerless in a state of fear, too. Get rid of a threat and you restore the balance of fear. Well, what that means for us, I won't presume to say. Just live and learn guys, learn and live."

I started to speak, but Joe stopped me, saying, "Just a minute, Wil. Here's the deal. I have another question about all this violence you've been told about. What about the war? Was there talk of any of that old standby accusation of treason?"

"I didn't hear a word about that theme this week. And I didn't think to ask. When Elwin was called a Wobbly, using that as a way to defame him, I imagine disloyalty is some of what they're saying. But I didn't hear it in any direct way this week. There's one more point of view I'd like to hear, one more about the lynch mob. I've heard about the barn dance and the fight from that person, but not that witness, that angle on the crime. And then I have to remember that I'm not here to investigate old evils. I'm supposed to be helping us hear the Good News, bring more folks to Jesus, and nurture our spiritual lives. If we figure out what really happened but nothing comes of it to help the survivors; if we can't help resolve things for a couple widows who remember, who are still troubled; if, if—then what's the use? And maybe it should help us understand better what Jesus was getting at when he saw the widow with her two coins."

"This discussion is getting too deep for me," Sherm said. "Wil, why don't you tell these guys what your little girl found on your drive through the back roads last Sunday."

So I told them about the adventure, how Ruthie found the tepee ring, and about things we learned as we explored. I related our talk with the kids about nomads. "Becca said, 'We moved. Are we nomads?' and I had to admit that maybe we are, but we hope not too soon again. I told them that my friend Joe thinks this land will make us nomads like it has for centuries."

By this time the men were starting to check wristwatches and glance at the wall clock. Instead of taking up his mantra of land and nomad, Joe said simply, "Thank you, Wil, for the appellation." He lifted his coffee mug in a toast. "Here's to friends. These guys are saying it's time to go. You better let them, Wil."

As Gary got up, he said, "I was expected at the Herald office ten minutes ago. If I go in with the headline, 'Five Year Old

Finds Tepee Rings on Jabbok Creek,' can I say I've been at work since 6:30?"

I replied, "Not without pictures. And I forgot to take my camera along."

Joe was still seated while others were going out the door. I wondered if he intended a lengthy dialogue. I didn't think I had time for that. But he stood then, and said, "This has been a good class, Wil. You better preach on something else, though. See you next week. And I do appreciate that we can call each other friends."

I didn't let him go without telling him that I'd met his niece. "You know what she calls you?"

"That I do. Sane Niece Janet has Crazy Uncle Joe figured out."

35

The youth group met at the church in mid-afternoon Sunday for a brief prep and a walk together to Prairie Manor for our young-meets-old party. Corey came in carrying a guitar case. They had more planned than I knew about.

As we reviewed our plans, I shared some of my recent discoveries with them. I told about a barn dance in 1918. Telling about trouble that had been stirred up with the combination of young men and alcohol reminded LeRoy and all of us that it isn't anything new and it can always lead to danger. I let the kids know that we would be visiting with people very special to me; one whose husband had been murdered the night of that barn dance party, and another person who had been at that party, who still feels the trouble it stirred in her family.

I couldn't be very clear in our short orientation session, but I had hopes that our bright, uncorrupted young people might bring something fresh into the conversations at the Manor. I now knew that they would also be bringing a little country music along with the cookies.

We left a note on the church door for Gordon and Todd, in case they might still arrive. As we walked the few blocks to the nursing home, Deb and Corey demonstrated that their

Halloween date had been a success. Now they were warming up their voices to sing a duet as they lagged behind the rest of us, walking hand in hand.

Dani said to me, "That's Madge Carter you talk to, isn't it."

"Yes, she's one I visit. I hope I didn't say too much to you all."

"She's a sweetie. I just love her. We brought her to church a few times." Then Dani said in a high pitched raspy voice, "I'm the oldest, you know." Her impersonation wasn't very accurate, but was amusing for all who heard her. Apparently Madge's signature line was as well-known here as Cronkite's "and that's the way it is" on TV news.

When we arrived at the Manor, Jennifer, Debbie and Dani went immediately to the big windows to look at the concrete wall mural. "Oh my gaw," said Jen, "that awful thing is still like that! Remember when we painted that?"

"Yeah, we were like in second or third grade. They shouldn't have to look at that still, should they," said Dani.

Debbie said, "Maybe we could get everyone who helped paint it before to do a better one."

"Do you have to make another big project for us?" Dani objected.

Jennifer said, "Well, it'll be a lot of work, but you have to admit, it needs a change. Let's see what Mr. Lahti thinks. And maybe Miss Fielder could get all the art classes into it."

They called Kevin and me over to look at the wall with them, and make their proposal. I said, "Let's visit with the folks for now. We can talk about this another time."

Kevin, however, was ready to jump on board with the girls' idea. "Pastor is right for now, but I'll talk with our art teacher. Ms. Fielder's art students might make a good design to blow up and paint. You'll have to work with the administrator here, too, you know. You say you all did this one when you were seven and eight?"

"Yeah, Mr. Lahti," said Debbie. "That's why I think the rest of the kids who're still around should help again. Make it better and just different."

Dani sighed. She knew that once her sister latched onto a project she wouldn't let go until it was done. And she knew that she'd be helping, like it or not.

From her nearby corner Madge overheard some of this conversation. Now she added her endorsement. "You girls painted on that wall, did you? Well, I'm sure that was kind of you, but I'm telling you now: I'm tired of it. And my old eyes can barely see it most days. I'm the..." And all three girls joined in a chorus with Madge, "...oldest, you know." And Madge laughed so hard it turned into a worrisome coughing fit.

A voice from the other end of the room shouted out, "She is not!"

I used the opening to give some directions. "Jen, Deb, why don't you go visit with the nay-sayer. I don't even know her name. See if you can get her on a more pleasant topic. And Dani and I are going to visit with Madge for a couple minutes."

From the corner of my eye, I saw Nilda come into the room then, and engage Corey in conversation, interrupting his guitar tuning. LeRoy, Steph and Stacy had gone with Julia to invite residents to come to the big room for music and cookies.

We approached Madge, set chairs near her that we each carried, and I did introductions. "Madge, do you remember Danielle? She says her family has given you a ride to church sometimes."

Before Madge could answer, Dani reached out to shake hands, saying, "Hello Mrs. Carter. You'd know me by Dani, not Danielle." She gave me a quick look saying by her expression that I shouldn't try to confuse Mrs. Carter.

"Are you one of the twins?" Madge asked. Dani nodded vigorously. Madge looked at me as she said, "My goodness. I remember two little look-alike girls. Has it been that long? She's all growed up."

"Debbie and I are not identical, you know."

"You are to these old eyes. My Buddy and Ralph are a year apart, but I've been calling them by the wrong name most of their lives. And my third boy is Peter. He says he grew up thinking his name was Buddyralphpeter."

"Madge," I said, "I told the young people a little of what you've been telling me about your family and things that happened. Not the whole story or anything, but some. I wonder what you'd want to tell Dani and her friends about the early days in Sage County and Harstad."

"What day was it that I told you about that night, about the killing, what that mob did to my Elwin?" said Madge.

I said, "That was just this past Tuesday, I think."

"You know, Pastor," she said, "that night, Tuesday you say, I only woke up once. And I didn't lay there awake in the dark at all, I went right back to sleep after….you know. Ever since I told you, I've been sleeping at night And in my chair here, too, like always. But I'm not fearful like I was."

"That's pretty amazing, isn't it, Pastor Wil," Dani said.

"Yes, it is." And, stepping into my preacher role, I paraphrased some holy scripture. "'My peace I give you,' said Jesus. 'Not as the world gives, so don't be afraid.'"

We heard some attention seeking noises behind us. Madge, who was already facing that direction, said to Dani, "That other copy of you wants something, Dear."

Dani growled, "Grrr. Why can't Deb let us be for two minutes. We were just started on a nice talk."

Deb did get our attention. She and Corey were ready to offer the song they'd been rehearsing for all of one short week. I got up to introduce our group and the two singers.

Corey struck a couple chords, looking back and forth from the music stand to his fingering, and Deb started to sing in a pure, thin soprano. I thought, we need a mike and amp for these old folks to hear her. Then Corey joined in with close harmony on "If I Needed You." Deb's volume picked up a little, and resonance picked up too. I thought I was hearing Emmylou herself. Corey's singing was light years ahead of his guitar skills, but that was okay, too. The audience showed so much appreciation that they decided to try another. The old Everly Brothers tune was less polished, but the kids seemed to be naturals at close harmony. Corey chorded the guitar with more confidence on a solo of "You've Got a Friend"—announced as a solo, but Deb managed some back-up anyway. Nilda had been listening from a seat at a dining table, and gave them a standing ovation, all by herself. Then she went over to Madge's corner and sat in the chair I had moved there.

I looked around the room, at the pleasant gathering. Steph and Stacy, the junior highs, were holding back, less engaged with the residents. Julia was with them, getting ready to serve cookies. Bless Stacy for making sure we brought something for the diabetics and special diets. Serving would have to wait for the activity aide to help us do that correctly.

LeRoy was talking with a tall elderly man wearing boots with riding heels and carrying a big hat. I hadn't seen him before. They were standing, talking beside a woman in a wheelchair who was a familiar resident. LeRoy saw me watching and beckoned me over. Corey and I joined them at the same moment.

LeRoy introduced Mr. Anderson as a great supporter of high school rodeo. Mr. Anderson was more interested in meeting the young musician.

Mr. Anderson said, "Howard Anderson, good to meet you Pastor Wilson, this is Frances, my wife. She stays here for now. Then he turned to Corey, "If you ever need a big old stand-up bass with a big old bass player to help you out, I know someone."

Frances said, "Oh, Howie, you think you can play the music the young folks like?"

"If they play that good country pop like we just heard? Yes, I can."

I was making the mental connections. Out loud I said, "Mr. Anderson, have you lived around here for long?"

He said, "Yeah, ranched out a little east of here all my life. What about it?

"Well, I'm becoming sort of a local history buff and I think there might be something you can help me figure out. Can we sit and visit sometime?"

"I don't know if I can help you much, but you can find me here mid-day, around dinner time most days. Unless Francie and I manage to go out."

"Thank you. I'll be in touch. I'll explain why I'm asking when we meet," I said, and excused myself to listen in at the Madge corner. Trays of cookies, coffee and juice were coming around. Serving had the younger girls making actual contact with the local populace.

With little room to move another chair in close, I found myself hovering over the group in Madge's favorite spot—a man intruding upon a ladies tea. Madge had appropriated a good place to sit, too. With sunshine at the right time of day, a panorama view from the patio to the front entryway, it was a place to watch the comings and goings while somewhat separated from them.

Dani, Deb & Jen were engaged in conversation with both Madge and Nilda. Madge and Nilda—together. That was so unexpected. It had me too curious to stay away. The conversation I heard kept me listening, trying not to intrude.

As I came near enough to hear, Madge was saying, "Girls, really, that's just sisterhood. It was no different when I was a girl."

Jen said, "Oh, I know I really shouldn't be jealous of all the attention Stacy gets. She sure didn't ask for diabetes. And all the good things she can't eat. But sometimes it gets me. She's always the center of attention, so I'll do something really awful. Like I'll eat a candy bar right in front of her. Then she goes whining to mom, and I feel real sorry and still mad at the same time. That's just not right, is it."

Dani and Deb were looking at each other now. It was Dani who spoke. "Is there any way ever to stop being jealous? I've been jealous of Deb forever. It's so easy for her to speak up, and get other people to do things. Now she has a boyfriend and I'm really jealous."

Deb's jaw dropped. "You say you're jealous, Dani? And here I was going to wait until we get home—you know, to get your advice like I always count on. I think maybe Corey and I are a better duet than a couple. And if I say that, he won't even want to sing with me. That part's so much fun. And we're good, too, aren't we."

"Yes you are! You see? Your sister is the one to keep close. I hope....no I trust, I truly believe that you'll grow out of those little tiffs between you," said Nilda. "Your sister will be your friend longer than anybody, if all goes well." She paused. As Jen started to respond, she held up her hand, saying simply "but" in a way that made it clear she had more to say. Jen stopped. We all waited in silence for a long moment. "But....but, does all go well? I suppose it does for some people. But what if..." And she shook her head, daubed at her eyes with a Kleenex, gave a little waving gesture with her fingers, and got very quiet.

After an awkward silence, Madge said. "Oh, Nilda, you do weigh yourself down. I see that. I look at you trudging down the hallway, poking the pastor with that big ole cane. Sure it never all goes well. I've outlived two husbands, a baby, and now my Buddy laying in the hospital in Rapid might go before me, too. Still and all, an awful lot went well, and it's enough. It's enough. So, I just get up in the morning, count the places that don't hurt—that don't take long anymore—and take pride that I'm....say it with me girls....I'm the oldest, you know."

And the girls did say it with her, and everybody had a laugh. We waited for the repudiator's shout, but she had disappeared right after cookies.

Then Madge had more to say. "As the oldest, let me give you girls some advice. Jennie, you eat those candy bars in hiding. Hear me? But a bright, pretty girl like you—just pay attention when you're getting attention. I bet you get lots. And you twins, see how you cherish each other? How can you miss. You tell that boy how you feel. Singing partners are a dime a dozen, but you can't pretend love. There, I've had my say, so don't say anything back at me. Humph."

"You make it sound like a young husband getting killed isn't so much worse than girls' growing up predicaments," said Nilda, who had been twitching in her chair. "And that's what it's about, see. Your first husband getting killed. Why I can't face you. Except I had to try today. And I'm going to get it out, one way or another. I know what happened. I know how Papa was shell-shocked almost like Walter was when he came back from the war. And, why oh why, wasn't there something I could've done?"

Madge was stunned. We all were. She asked, finally, "What did you do?"

"Nothing!" Nilda nearly shouted, then dropped to little more than a whisper. "That's just it. I should've stood in the way, said something to stop Papa from going with those men."

"How could you know, dear?" asked Madge, in a choking whisper.

Nilda closed her eyes. She gave no spoken answer. They, and we, had run out of words. I wiped my eyes and looked around. First at the girls, so unusually quiet, then toward the entryway where I saw that the rest of our group milling about. Kevin caught my eye and pointed at his wristwatch. As the responsible adult, I had to urge the young women to join the others for a walk back to the church and some de-briefing. As we drew away, Nilda and Madge were sitting in silence. Madge held both of Nilda's hands in hers.

As soon as we hit the sidewalk outside, Jennifer said for all of us, "That was amazing!" We walked on, mostly without speaking. LeRoy stayed on the edge of the group, just as he had throughout our time at the Manor. Corey tried to share his excitement about the music, but got little response from the girls he most wanted to impress. The younger girls, Steph and Stacy, expressed the adulation he sought, but were non-committal about their experience. When I asked them if they had a good time with the old folks, they answered, "It was okay."

As we neared the church Debbie said, "Don't forget. We have to get Miss Fielder to help with painting that old wall."

"How do you do it?" Dani asked her sister. "After all that was going on with those incredible old ladies, how can you even remember that wall?"

I closed that debate before it went further by saying, "Mysteries of the human mind, Dani, mystery of the mind."

When we arrived back at the church, parents were waiting, impatient at our lateness. We needed our reflection time, but it would have to wait. For now we'd settle for a circle song and prayer with parents enlarging the circle. The prayer, which included needs of our teens with siblings and jealousies, our elderly friends with burdens of old conflicts seeking redemption, also contained the ulterior motive that parents might ask their kids what those prayers were really about.

***

That evening, while Berta got the girls to bed and stories read, I brought my journal up from the cold basement study, opened it in my lap, pushed back in the recliner, and closed my eyes to consider for a moment how I could record the events of the afternoon. I woke up hearing Berta as she got up to turn off the TV. She suggested that I might be more comfortable sleeping in bed. The journal, still on my lap, was set aside and I stumbled after her.

36

On Monday morning I tried again to write some notes about the previous afternoon. Now the first questions were on the order of, "What actually happened? How much of my memory is real and how much imagined?" As I wrote, I knew that I wanted to visit with Nilda right away, but also had a feeling I should wait a day—one of those gut feelings that come, without a clear reason, but that I was learning to pay attention to. So, I waited until Tuesday afternoon, the time I'd be expected at the Manor anyway.

I arrived at Prairie Manor so early that Nilda wasn't yet waiting in the entryway to greet me with her cane. I found her sitting in her room staring out at the park. Her deep chair had been turned a few degrees so that she could look out the window more easily. With the bed in the way this would make it more difficult to position the straight-back chair for eye contact and conversation. I called a greeting from the open doorway.

Nilda responded, "And good afternoon to you, Pastor Wil. Help me up and you can turn this chair so I can see you."

So much for my fleeting conspiracy thought. She really did want to look out the window. It was not about avoiding eye contact. We moved the furniture a few inches and sat down for a visit.

"You came early," she said. "You want to hear everything I haven't told you, I suppose."

"Well, there's some of that, alright," I answered. "But also I want to know if there's more I can help you with, uh, about what's going on now, too. I was surprised and pleased, I guess, to see you with Madge. Surprised at the things you were saying to her on Sunday."

She said, "We've been talking like this, most every week, haven't we. And there's something you said in your sermon that morning. Now I can't remember. Isn't that strange? I can't remember, but it gave me courage. That and our talks. But there was something that urged me to go ahead that very day. And those young ladies made it easier, too. I don't know how. Those are some fine girls, Pastor. Help them all you can. I can't imagine what the young folks are facing. Not like when I was young."

"Well, it is different in some ways," I said. "But it's the same in others, you know. Some kids will face difficulties, just as you have. And be tough enough to survive, like you. Some will have troubles they can't handle, I'm afraid. Others will have it easy all through life, I expect. But we all need help from one another, and I'll do the best I can with what little wisdom God has given me."

"Oh, you are a blessing, Pastor." Then she said, "One thing we need right now is a cup of coffee, since I've had my after dinner rest now. You know where the coffee pot is, don't you. Go get us some, if you will. That'll be a blessing, too."

I got the coffee, black the way I like it. I didn't remember how Nilda liked hers, but she accepted it black without a word. Once seated again, I said, "You told us the other day that your father was somehow connected with the mob on the night Mr. Bowdler was killed. Or was it a posse?"

"A posse. Hmm. A posse." She sat musing for a long moment. "Now you mention it, I believe that's what I thought it was. When Papa left with the other men, I thought they were intent on bringing the man back. They did believe that he had attacked George, poor George. You know, he did recover from that blow. I heard he was drinking and picking fights way over to Mott just a few months after."

"You thought it was a posse, but it really wasn't?" I asked, to get back on track.

"I thought they were going to get Madge's husband. I didn't know Madge then, of course. Just for that one day. I thought it was about getting at the truth. To find out how George got hurt, and maybe I knew it was really about the League or the Wobblies or whatever it really was he was selling. But I thought they just needed to talk to him, let the sheriff talk to him. What I didn't know was that a group had already gone out for that purpose. Papa was with the second group. They were all about stopping the League, taking care of the problem so Kirchen wouldn't get like Plentywood, with the Communists stirring trouble all around. That's what I'd been told the League was. How could I know any different? I thought it was a posse for the law. And I didn't stop Papa. I didn't want him to go, but could I say so? Anyway, he went out, right from the Lintner's. In the middle of the night."

"And you and the rest of your family went home then?"

"Not until the morning. There was a lot of us stayed at Lintner's. Most in the barn or camping out. Mom, Magda and I stayed in the house.

"Now here's the thing. There's some things I didn't know 'til years later. Papa told me things about that night when he was sick and thought he was about to die. Used me for a deathbed confession, he did. And then he got better, never well, but better. He didn't want to, but he lived for another year before he succeeded in dying. He thought he was dying and he told me things. Of course Walt was mad as all get out that he let me take Maggie and Junior home for two weeks and Papa didn't even die."

"Succeeded in dying?" I asked.

"That's what Herb, my brother, said—when I asked him how Papa died. He said, 'Let's just say he succeeded. He got what he wanted.' That's all I know."

We finished our coffee before she continued. "There's lots I forget, but this I remember. Papa said the word went among the men about how we have to stop that Wobbly, spreading his socialist philosophy, and he might've killed George. When Papa told it, it sounded like he didn't really believe that the man— that's Madge's husband—had anything to do with what happened to George. But that was what everybody was saying, and they were going after him. They kept up that kind of talk late into the night. They got George patched up and Sam and Mrs. Fenton—their mother—got him to town and Dr. Schneider. After that they were fired up for action. So Papa says he went along. They all piled onto a pickup truck. I saw that myself, those men heading out from Lintner's, weighing that Model T so the springs were flat, bouncing out of the farmyard. Papa said the talk was so angry and he just got caught up in the anger they boiled up together. George being hurt just turned it into this big mad wrath about agitators, coming in stirring up trouble, tearing the Kirchen community apart. So Papa was part and parcel in the killing that night. At least he regretted it later. Of course that regret turned him into a sad, sad man. Sad and secretive for the rest of his short life. Is there any way I can leave the Franks and Ruud family sadness before I die? But maybe that's what heaven is for."

Still troubled by what 'succeeded in dying' really meant, now I saw in her last question and theological musing an invitation to a word of grace. I was still figuring out how I might say it when she got back to her story.

"Papa said they were in North Dakota when they met the sheriff coming back with the prisoner. The sheriff later claimed he was sure that night that he never left Montana. But they were in Dakota, alright. So there they were, out on that wagon track along the section line, Sheriff Harney's Dodge headed west and that truck full of angry men facing east, and the road in between lit up by the headlights. And this is what Papa told me, that day he thought he was dying. He said, 'That's when I said the words I have ever since wanted to swallow back down.

That's when I said what I never should've spoken. The tongue is a fire. In the heat of anger, I spoke before I thought.' My Papa said all that and more when he was fixing to die. He told me what he said that night. And that was all it took."

I was on the edge of the chair leaning forward, waiting to hear those fateful words. As I waited I began to worry that she might announce that it's time for a prayer and call it a day. Instead, Nilda finally stated the source of her hesitation. "After Papa got better, when he didn't die right away, he swore me to secrecy. I know I have to tell you, but it is a betrayal. Papa didn't want his blame said out loud."

"Was that promise for while he was alive?" I asked. "It seems from the way you've told it that he needed it kept secret for his reputation while he was alive. It's a long time since."

"Well, that's my hope, Pastor Wil. And if it's sin, then you're in it, too." She took in a long slow breath, and said, "Papa told me of the time when he and those other men jumped out of the truck to meet Sheriff Harney and the men with him. He told me what he said. 'Back home they'd know how to handle this.' Papa claimed he didn't even know what he meant by that, but that was all it took. One of the others said, 'We'll handle this right now.' And a Model 12 Winchester came out of the cab and those men just walked around the sheriff, pulled Mr. Bowdler out of the back of that big Dodge and held him to the ground on the bank of the barrow pit. And the sheriff, Mr. Harney, he didn't even argue. In fact, Papa said, he seemed relieved. Even when they heard the gun being pumped, and then another. Two shots fired, one right after the other. The man tied at his wrists and ankles, trying to crawl up the bank on his back. Killed. In cold blood."

Nilda shuddered and daubed at the tears welling up. She still had more to say. "Papa wouldn't or couldn't say who the shooters were. And that officer of the law, standing right there looking at it, and didn't see a thing. It was dark, don't you know. How Madge can put that all behind her like she does, I'll never know."

I started to say that she hasn't, but realized that could wait a little while.

"That sheriff, didn't see a thing was his testimony later. That night, according to Papa, all he said was, 'That's one less Wobbly to worry about.' And he got in his car. They turned the Ford around, the men piled in again, and they all drove on back, some to the Lintner spread, Mr. Harney went on into Harstad. And all Papa ever said later was, 'don't speak of it again.' And now I have." She looked up to the ceiling and added, "Papa, forgive me. Understand. Now I know Madge, and it had to be told."

With that Nilda stopped, gently slapped her knees as finishing gesture, then reached her hands toward me, palms up, and said, "Let's pray now."

***

When I left Nilda's room, a few minutes still remained before our singing group would arrive. As we walked together to the big room, I said, "I think I'll visit with Madge for a few minutes. Singers aren't due yet."

Nilda said, "Thanks for asking, but I won't join you." (I hadn't asked.) "I'm worn out now, so I'll just sit in my usual place and listen to the singing."

Madge was sound asleep in her comfy chair in the corner. This day there was an empty chair pushed close to hers, so I sat down and tried to wake her gently. It took a loud, "Hello, Madge."

She startled awake and said, "Why Pastor Ti...Wil. It's good to see you again. Here I am, sleeping the day away, so I can lay awake all night. Did I tell you I was sleeping better?"

"Yes. You seemed to have unburdened by telling your most difficult memories."

"Well, that didn't last long. Now I wake up with worries about right now. Buddy is still in the hospital in Rapid City. He's not getting any better, they tell me. Might be they'll pull the plug and just let him die. I'm ready. Why not me? Well, of course I thought that way long, long ago when Maralta died.

She was just a baby, one year old. And I can't go see my Buddy or anything. Then if I'm not fretting or praying for Buddy, I'm thinking about our Nilda over there. What she was telling me. Why does she burden herself with the blame? Can you tell me a reason? It just makes no sense to me."

"Buddy will be in my prayers, too," I said. "I don't know what to say. It's so hard when you can't even be there with him, I know. A parent wants to be able to do something. And I'm sorry your sleep is uneasy again. But then you asked a hard question, and I don't know the reason. Maybe these feelings don't need reasons. Might even be similar to what I said a moment ago. You want to be able to do something, or to go back in time and fix it. Whatever the reason or the need, the burden has been there. What I'd like us to do, if we can, is I'd like to get the three of us together and see what comes out of it. I know that our friend Nilda needs to have that burden lifted. And I think that you and I can help."

"Oh, Pastor, you sound like you're starting to burden yourself too much, too. I suppose if I can't be where I think I should, as the old mom, maybe God wants me here for another purpose. So, bring her on over. I can't promise I'll say the right thing, or not say the most wrong thing for that matter, but call her on over."

Just then Rachel and a couple more singers came bustling in, with happy greetings for everyone they passed on the way to the piano. Before I made any move to help pull the piano out from the wall, I said to Madge, "Today Nilda told me a lot of what happened, from her perspective. And that wore her out, so even if the singers hadn't come in just now, we needed to wait. I'll come back later in the week. Right now, though, we better bow our heads and have a prayer." I got us into a visibly obvious prayer posture so they wouldn't get after me for not helping with the piano. We prayed for Buddy, his caregivers, for Nilda and Madge, for acceptance and peace.

And we sang, with gusto but not well. I couldn't help thinking about the really good singing the kids had provided just two days earlier.

37

Harstad made a big production of Veteran's Day. Wednesday was marked with a program of readings and speeches beginning at eleven o'clock sharp in the high school auditorium. The American Legion and Masonic Lodge jointly sponsored the program. Tradition demanded that a junior high student who was good at memorizing would recite the Gettysburg Address. Stacy was that student this time and, as the new preacher in town, I was tapped to give an invocation. As I prepared earlier that morning, I had a momentary desire to make the prayer into a speech recalling the day's origins in World War I armistice, and the trauma that veterans of that war carried long after. I wanted to challenge the current folks with their history in the way dissenters and German language speakers were treated. Caught up in the stories of the killing in 1918 as I was, I had to check myself, and pray along with the people actually present. So, I wrote notes for one prayer into my journal and a complete text of another for delivery at the program.

After the program many of us found our way to the hall at the fairgrounds for pot-luck—pot-luck except that the pork ribs and baron of beef were provided by the sponsors. As Berta and

I got into the long line, I noticed Howard Anderson, the old cowboy whom I wanted to consult, about ten people ahead of me. As he came away from the buffet table I watched to see where he'd sit, hoping we might find places near enough that I could ask my questions over lunch. Tables were filling fast, but we still managed to score a couple spots on the bench nearly across from Mr. Anderson. Then, to my surprise, Sophie Kettle appeared and the men at the long table made room for her to squeeze in more directly across from him.

Sophie got seated and plowed ahead with unneeded introductions. "Mr. Anderson, have you met Pastor Wilson and his wife Roberta? Wil, this is Howard Anderson. You should convince him to talk to you about the old days. He's got some great stories that might help you with your investigation."

"It's investigation now, is it? Listening to the remembrances was always supposed to be pastoral care," I said. "Have I lost sight of that so completely?"

My question was ignored by both, but Berta said, knowingly, "Could be."

"I have met the pastor, Mrs. Kettle. Nice to meet you Mrs. Wilson." Howard said. "Wil and I met at the Manor the other day when I was spending some time with Francie. And the good pastor approached me just like you did. 'Tell us about the old days.'" He almost sang that sentence. "Makes me suspicious. Did you already tell him what I told you, Sophie?"

I spoke up before Sophie could answer. "Sophie and I have swapped a few tidbits from a few different sources, but Sophie doesn't say who says what." Sophie nodded, affirming my statement. I went on, "So, was it you, who told her about the party at the Lintner Ranch? In fact, she didn't know the name of the ranch. It was your mention of a bass violin. When you offered the kids some backup on bass fiddle, I remembered being told—not by Sophie—about a tall kid who played in the band that day. And that made me think you might have something to add to what I've been learning."

"Hey, I do hope to jam with those kids. That girl will really have a voice with just a little more maturing. How can I get a hold of them?"

"I'll tell them you really mean it," I said. "And that you have some musical wisdom that can help them. Their friend LeRoy knows how to get ahold of you, right?"

"Yeah, you tell them. I'm in the book," he said, then turned back to the other issue. "Why the hell does that 1918 mess keep coming up? The Lintner party. That's more than fifty years ago. Okay, it's too bad somebody had to die, but we never had any more trouble with the Wobblies or Commies. Not like they had up north, or over in Dakota with that so-called Nonpartisan crap."

"Well, Mr. Anderson, I wonder...," I said. "I wonder if some of that isn't why it still resonates among us today. I know some who absolutely have not gotten over it. But, you're right that it settled down some of the conflicts around here. But that leaves a legacy, I have to think. A legacy that affects the way we face, or bury, issues today."

"Give us an example, then," Howard demanded.

"Well, that's my problem. I have this feeling about it that I just can't shake, but I don't have anything concrete to prove it. So, maybe it's just me, and I'll have to live here awhile to figure it out. Maybe I have it all wrong."

Sophie backed me up. "I hear what Wil is saying, I think. I kind of get a feeling like that, too. I can't quite put my finger on it, but it makes me want to know more."

"A friend told me a while back," I said, "that to understand Harstad and Kirchen County I need to learn about the Nonpartisan League and about the Odessa Germans during the First World War. I may not have examples for you, other than individuals directly impacted by the killing that night, but I think my friend is right."

"That was then. This is now," Howard asserted. "Now this town runs on oil and gas. Altogether different, whatever Joe might say. I was doomed to grow up in interesting times. How about you? Don't we all bear that curse in one way or another? But I can't accept that we're doomed by the times almost seventy year ago. Do you really believe that, Mr. Man-of-God?"

"What makes you think my friend's name is Joe?" I did not point out that it had been Cal who gave that advice. "Anyway, to respond to your question, I believe...,"

"The question was rhetorical for now. I'm not done yet. You young folks, the ones they call the boomer generation, you all think 1968 was the most important year since baby Jesus. Well, let me tell you. 1918 was another of those years. Influenza, war, Bolsheviks in Russia, the prohibition movement was growing full steam, and our neighbors to the east were all in for their Nonpartisan League. Nonpartisan my ass. It was all politics all the time for Townley and his gang. And all for Townley, I might add. So, yes, our German folks had a time, new prejudices come with war. And old prejudices come out of hiding, too. What do you think it's like for a young kid who just wants to impress the girls by making music in a year like that? And you want to understand who we are today because of one summer night? Well, I was there. I didn't see anything until they were calling for help and we stopped playing, right in the middle of an allemande left. All I saw was George laying on the ground, out cold with blood all over his scalp. They said the Wobbly from Sage did it, whacked him with a rock. I never heard of a Wobbly until that night. And that's all I know about that night. I heard the next day that he got killed. Don't know how, don't know who. End of rant."

With that Mr. Anderson took a last bite off a bar-b-q rib, picked up his paper plate and headed for the trash can and the door.

"Whoa," I said, "we got an earful and no chance to respond. Do you think he made his point of the events back then being so different from today, Sophie?"

"Maybe the opposite," Sophie answered. "Of course we're not cursed. Affected, but not cursed by an earlier interesting time. You haven't claimed that, have you? But the influence is with us, and his diatribe demonstrates it, as far as I'm concerned."

"Yes, the influence. The way I see it, every community has a personality of its own. And for good or ill, most likely both, once that personality is formed, it stays with us. Part of my role needs to be in helping to make it for good more than ill, I believe. Knowing the past is necessary to being faithful in the present." I asked finally, "See what I'm saying?"

"I think so," Sophie replied. "For instance, for the German background folks in your flock, their need to honor that heritage is more important because of 1918. Does that go with what you're saying?

"Uh-huh," I said. "And it looks like lunch is over. Everybody's leaving, and I need to get some things ready for Wednesday Church School. It may be a holiday, but as long as school is in session, so are we. Good to visit with you. I think Mr. Anderson had the best speech of the day. Although, I would like a chance to defend myself."

"Not that you actually would," Berta said as she maneuvered off the bench. "We better go and get Becca. Mary Ann is probably at her wits end by now."

"It's probably just as well you didn't try to defend yourself, Rev. The speech in the program was nice and patriotic, but bland by comparison. See you." Sophie got up, grabbing all our plates and went to discard them and visit with the kitchen clean-up crew.

We drove home. I left the Renault there so that Berta could bring our girls to church school later, and walked to the church.

38

The mild weather we were enjoying ended with winter's sudden return Friday morning. I backed the old car through three inches of new snow on the driveway, skidded to the opposite curb and crept across town to the Men's breakfast. It was later than our starting time, but only Sherm had beat me to the café. Others straggled in, stomping wet snow off their boots and complaining about the slippery conditions over the next fifteen minutes. Cal and Joe came in together. Joe murmured as he shook the snow off his jacket, "Forecast called for a few flurries. Must be our Friday the 13th curse."

Karl announced what Sherm had already told us—that Ed wouldn't be with us because he'd taken on a contract to plow parking lots at Super Valu and the bank. Gary blew in just as breakfast plates were set in front of Sherm and me. Others gave Sally their orders and we were finally ready to start.

"You better have joke this week, Gary. You've been letting us down lately." said Sherm.

"Well, be let down then, Sherm. What I have is a cartoon, but not a funny one," Gary replied. "I was digging through a box of college course notes. You know, tossing out lecture notes that I never want to see again, or can't figure what the hell they even say. Anyway, I found what I was really looking for, which was the stuff from a course about newspaper writing in North Dakota history. So I have a cartoon from the Nonpartisan Leader for you."

Gary looked at me and added, "I've been holding out on you, Wil. I didn't want to say what I know about the League because I forgot most of it right after the final exam, and the rest I forgot before the test."

Gary unfolded the cartoon and smoothed it on the table. It showed a man and woman in pilgrim garb. The man labeled 'N Dak farmer', the woman 'North Dakota'. The man had a blunderbuss over his shoulder labeled 'political power'. Gary said, "This is your Thanksgiving card, since I won't be here next week."

"Can you explain it, Gary?" I asked.

"Well, only that this is an example of the illustrations that the Nonpartisan Leader used to remind the farmers what they were accomplishing, and keep them committed to the program." Gary addressed the whole group, saying, "The Leader was the weekly news rag put out by the League from about 1915 to '22 or so. What I do know from my time at ND State is that most all the newspapers in those days were biased screeds that only published what the editor agreed with. So there were other papers that always presented the NPL as the work of the devil."

"Wow," I said, "You really have been holding out on us, Gary. All our talk about the League and you just sat there."

"Tell you what, Wil. When I get a chance, I'll bring you my notes and the handouts. I have a few samples copied from the old papers."

"I think we'd all like to see what you've got, Gary," Joe said.

I knew that 'we all' really meant Cal and Joe, so I said, "Why don't we have Gary call us together, Joe. Maybe we can look at his copies and stuff over at the library. I suspect Ms. Kettle might be interested, too. Are you into this, too, Cal?"

"I am. Give me a call whenever," he answered.

"Anyone else?" Heads shook. I looked at the clock. "Are you watching the time, Cal?"

"No work for me today. I'm lucky enough to have a job that isn't worth the risk when it's this slick. Friday the 13th can be good luck, don't you know."

"Well then, we'll look forward to hearing from Gary," I said. "What's next? You all want the Bible lesson or would you rather hear about the killing? I've been learning all about it this week."

"Whatever. You're the boss," Karl said.

"Yeah right," was my retort. "The lesson in Mark has a couple verses that really go with what came before, of his teaching at the temple, and then a little apocalyptic message." I put a quarter on the table next to Sherm's coffee mug. "And since what I'm thinking about is how the killing in 1918 affects our community, I'm inclined to stick with those first couple verses today. Then I'll still have to figure out what to do on Sunday.

"So, here's what it says in Mark chapter thirteen, verses one and two.

And as he came out of the temple, one of his disciples said to him, "Look, Teacher, what wonderful stones and what wonderful buildings!" And Jesus said to him, "Do you see these great buildings? There will not be left here one stone upon another, that will not be thrown down."

"Okay Rev, this I got to hear," Cal said. "How can that possibly apply to our local story. He's talking about the temple, which was destroyed about the time Mark was writing. Isn't that right?"

"That is right, Cal," I said. I'm doing some blatant allegory or something. Questionable as all get out. If you let me do it now, I'll try to avoid it on Sunday, okay?"

Joe gave the response. "As one never given to fanciful ideas..." And Cal gave him a pretended slap upside the head that didn't actually touch him. "I say tell us what you're thinking so we can sort it out."

"A man was killed by a mob in 1918. They called him a Wobbly, radical unionist, but he was really an ordinary farmer, who was trying to help an organization of farmers pulling together. They were gaining enough power in North Dakota that the state was taking some important functions like grading, milling, and storing wheat away from the corporation owners in the Twin Cities. So the railroad and business people in Montana wanted to stop it before it could really get started here. What I've been hearing leads me to believe that the killing was part of that. An angry mob got stirred up to stop the organizer. It went too far and Elwin Bowdler was dead.

"Don't people always pile stones into something we would see as a thing of beauty. Sometimes the stones are real bricks, but sometimes they are ideas or religion or corporate shares. Jesus is going all out here, I think. He says yep, it's lovely but it cannot last. The structures we build will fall to ruin, and he says he has something more to offer. Something that killing it to make it go away won't stop. Or pulling the chief keystone to topple the arch won't close the gateway to the full life he brings." It occurred to me that I was preaching, which I didn't intend at breakfast, so I stopped.

"Don't shy away from saying that to your congregation, Preacher," Joe said. "Are you saying that motivation where one gets killed or just taken out of the picture in order to keep us together and docile is in the religion that Jesus was up against? And your Christian claim is that Jesus shows it doesn't really work? I still can't get my head around this Easter thing. It just defies too much of nature for me. Is that the deal? Is that what it's about for you?"

"I guess. Yeah, that's exactly what I'm saying. Thank you for clearing that up, because I didn't know I was saying that until you said it." I said this while at the same time trying to write some notes on our dialogue. I put down my pen and added, "And the connection to so many killings in every age strikes me. Think of all the different take-aways from the Bowdler killing. The general memory of the event is that he was an IWW radical who attacked another man at the barn dance. So the mob killed him before the sheriff could get him to jail. And the sheriff approved. Some witnesses at the scene say he wasn't involved in a fight at all, that the other man was injured in a drunken fall while fighting his own brother. But still the common claim is that it took care of a problem and the community conflict was eased after that. Of course, the Armistice—we just had Vet's Day—the Armistice came just a few months later, too. But I'm coming around to the idea that the killing that night long ago didn't settle anything. It just hid it, and we still live with it. It's part of who we are as a community. What I'm struggling with now, is what we do with that knowledge."

"Maybe there's nothing we can do," Cal said. "And I'm not saying I even agree with you. But right or wrong, this town doesn't move fast, so tread carefully, Pastor Wil."

Karl and Sherm were nodding agreement. Gary was imitating Cal's late for work, jump and run routine. We all looked at the clock then and Karl said, "If we stay much longer we'll have to order some lunch." The snow was still coming down and blowing into drifts, so we left the deep discussion to brave the deep snow on the streets.

***

I tried to preach it that Sunday. I had worked over the ideas while the snow piled up on Friday, and re-written early Sunday morning. By then the sermon was so academic that even the preacher didn't understand the point. It was a relief and pleasure to spend part of the afternoon in the brisk sunshine with Cal, Henry, LeRoy and Corey shoveling the heavy snow from driveways for some older folks. Having Corey show up with LeRoy let me encourage him arrange a jam session with Mr. Anderson, assuring him that the old man's offer was genuine and could be helpful and fun.

39

Two phone calls came on Monday, one right after the other, just before noon. The first was Madge's son Peter, calling from Rapid City, telling me that his brother Bertram had died. He wanted me to deliver the news to their mother.

Before I could get my coat the second call came, this time from the RN on duty at the Manor. She called to tell me of Peter's request that I come, and to say that she was advising them that Madge wasn't strong enough to travel to South Dakota. Now I felt a sense of urgency about the task before me.

I arrived at Prairie Manor in the midst of bustling and movement. Tables were being cleared, scrubbed and arranged after the noon dinner meal. Wheelchairs were rolling through the hallways around slowly moving walkers. Madge's comfy chair was empty, so I headed for her room. Nilda saw me and waved her cane at me as I turned the corner. I just waved back and kept moving. I found Madge working her walker toward her room with an aide at her side. I steered myself ahead of them so that Madge could see me, and after a greeting said to the aide, "Would you like me to see Madge to her room?"

"No," she said, "I need to help her for just a minute or two. Then you can visit." I realized what she meant and waited outside the door.

The aide came out, nodded to me and I went in. Madge was settled in her chair and another chair was positioned just where I'd have put it. She was wearing her burgundy running suit, with a zippered sweatshirt that had a collar. And a pearl necklace. Other than a gold wedding band, worn down to little more than a wire, I had never seen Madge with any jewelry. She saw my stare fixed on the pearls.

"There's something I have to tell you, Madge," I said.

"Oh. My Buddy." And tears filled her eyes. "My Bertram is dead."

As I handed her a tissue I said, "Yes. It was early this morning. Peter called me a little while ago. He said that Buddy was hardly conscious ever since that last heart attack."

"You were looking at my pearls. It was Mother's Day. A few months after Mr. Carter,... after Charles died. My kids all got together and gave me these. So I put them on this morning after Buddy woke me up. Gave me such a start, he did. I was snoozing and there he was, saying it's okay. And then I was wide awake and he was gone. So I knew he'd died and I put on the pearls for my kids. "

I was speechless for a moment. Then, because I had no words of direct response, I said, "I'm told that travel to the funeral would be too exhausting for you. Peter said that Ralph and Cynthia are there, and Pearl is on her way. He also told me to tell you that Ralph would stop here for a day or two on his way home."

"What about Henry and Ruth? Did he say anything about them?" she asked with rising anxiety in her voice.

"He didn't. And not knowing any of them, I didn't think to ask."

"Pastor, do you suppose that's why I'm still around while my children go and die before me? Do you suppose I have to be here until I can get my brats to get along? There was always a coldness between my two families. I'll never understand it."

"I can't help you understand it. I just know it happens, and that you aren't responsible. I have no experience of it, and pray I never will, but I do know that losing a child is about the hardest thing. Seeing your baby die had to be just awful. And this is too, I suspect." I might have said more. I was saying things that might have made things worse instead of better. At least she knew we cared.

"I knew it was coming," she said, finally. "And I knew when it happened. Surprised the hell out of me. And I'm not apologizing for that word, neither. I really mean it. Hell has been surprised out of me. I know which way I'm going, and it is good. Just like God said at the Creation. It is good."

"Amen." Then I added, "Will you pray with me now?"

"I will, Wil. But let me start." She launched into a prayer of caring for her family, of hope for their future, and the promise of heaven that would leave my uncertain mumblings in the dust.

When my turn came the only thing I could add was, "In Jesus' name." I was noticing some movement at the door while we prayed.

At the 'amen' I looked over and saw Nilda with head bowed, hands folded over her cane, waiting in the doorway. Then she knocked while saying, "Madge, it's Nilda. Hello, Pastor. May I come in?"

I stood, helped Nilda into my chair and pushed another side chair from the still unused roommate area.

Nilda must have been at the open door longer than I realized. She took hold of Madge's hand and said, "I'm so sorry about your loss."

Madge's first reaction was to take offense. "How did you hear about that? Pastor just now told me."

"I was just passing by and I overheard." Nilda seemed crushed by her reaction, but Madge was undeterred.

"Your hearing's not that good. You were eavesdropping, weren't you."

I thought it might be time to intervene. "Some news just travels faster than light. Nilda certainly didn't want to add to your upset. She knows about grief and pain, too, and wanted to comfort."

"Oh? I'm sorry," said Madge. "It's just... Well, you understand, I'm not myself today."

"Well, of course not," I said. Thinking I should say more but not knowing what, I let it go.

Nilda seemed to be in a bit of speechless shock, too.

Madge then asked Nilda, "Have you had a child who died? I know you have a daughter who lives right here in Harstad. So you get to see her all the time."

Madge probably knew that Nilda frequently complained that Magda didn't visit often enough.

Wisely, Nilda responded only to the question. "No, I haven't lost a child in death. I have a son who won't speak to me and I don't know why."

It confused me, but I was beginning to feel like I must be there as some sort of broker. That led me to intrude into the dialogue. "This'll without a doubt be obvious to you two, but I've been learning some things and I haven't had to face what you have by any means. But it seems to me that there are all kinds of grief situations, and we all grieve our own way. You have each faced trials and come out on top. They are different, but not less or more, are they. We each get our own, don't we?"

"You are young, aren't you, Pastor," Madge said, then continued. "Of course you're right, but today is my turn, don't you know."

"Oh my, that is certainly so," I said. "And we pray that you'll get back the joy that shines out from your soul, your center. Now, since we're all here, Nilda and I are going to try to distract you anyway."

"We are?" asked Nilda.

"Listen now, I've lived a long time. Too long. I've buried two husbands, a baby, and now my oldest son. Bertram, my Buddy, who we always counted on. He was always there to take charge when no one else could. Now he's gone and I'm going to grieve and you can't stop me." Madge seemed to be gaining strength as she spoke.

"No, I sure don't want to get in the way of the mourning you need to do," I said, "but I need to tell you a bit about Nilda's, too. She's been telling me of her struggle, and your history is part of hers, too."

"Oh, that's right," said Madge. "We were talking about that when your group of young folks from the church was here."

"You have such an amazing memory, Madge," I said. "Not just the old times, but things you were told, things so easy to forget. But one little hint, and you remember. Anyway, it is that. The grief that Nilda has lived with, a father changed by a traumatic event, living with a sorrow that affected the whole family. Then her husband comes back from the war with the same kind of constant pain. What they called shell shock. So she's lived with a kind of grief without the death. Nilda's father apparently knew the truth but couldn't say it. The story that put the blame on Elwin was just too much to confront. They had to excuse the killing. And her Papa was in the mob, so he just held it in. And Nilda has told me, and maybe she's already told you, how she thinks she could have done something to prevent it."

"Just a minute, Wil," Nilda said. "I do see now that there really wasn't anything. I just hated what happened to my family. I wanted to pray it all better, and we just drifted on. And I look at Madge, who lost so much more, and see her looking happy, making jokes, so full of life no matter how old. I want things made right between us, for the sake of our families. Or for the sake of our memories, maybe. I had to come and be with you in your sorrow today. Maybe it would let me find something I'm missing."

"You sure have carried a chunk of hell on your shoulders, Nilda. I don't suppose you'll believe me, but Buddy appeared to me early this morning, just after he died," Madge said. "He says it's beautiful. So we shouldn't worry now, should we."

"A chunk of hell. That says it. A chunk of hell," Nilda said. "How can you see it so clear? How do you do it?"

"Nilda dear, I've been to hell and I wasn't going to live my whole life there."

"What a great attitude for life," I said. "Shows the kind of stamina we see in you."

"It took some time, you know," Madge began. "After the killing we were all in hell, me and my kiddos. I tried to look after them. They tried to look after me. And none of us did it too good. It wasn't until we were put off the land. That's when I decided I wasn't going to live in hell no longer. We loved that pretty Dakota farm, but it was a chunk of our hell by then. So we came to Montana. When Maralta died it took me most of a year to remember that I wasn't going to live in hell. And I've been working at it ever since. Now I'm the oldest and I can thank you both for reminding me. Buddy is off to heaven and I'm torn up today, but I'm not going to stay in no grief-hell."

"Oh, bless you, Madge. On such a sad day, and still I feel a load being lifted," Nilda said. "Will you forgive me?"

"Forgive you? For living too long in hell? If you've forgiven yourself, dear, God'll take care of the rest." With that Madge closed her eyes and was suddenly sound asleep with her head drooping forward. Nilda and I each put a hand on Madge's hands, had a short prayer and left the room. A nurse's aide was just coming down the hall, so we asked him to check on her.

As we walked slowly to the other wing where Nilda lived, she continued to ask about forgiveness. "How do I forgive myself?"

A wise counselor might have left her to work with that question by herself for a while. Lacking wisdom, I tried to answer with advice. "You've worried about what you might've done, said it in a way that you feel guilty. I don't think it's really guilt that keeps you troubled. It's something else. So, I wonder. Do you need to forgive your father? And Walter? Well, both Walters, for that matter."

We reached her room. At the door she said simply, "I need to rest now. Thanks for being here."

"Well, good-bye then, Nilda. I'll be here with the singers tomorrow."

"Good-bye, Pastor Wil."

40

When Berta asked after Madge that afternoon, all I could manage was to fuss about trying to be the wise counselor when the discovery of forgiveness might be working itself out in spite me. I set out to be God's messenger of healing to broker the peace, to enable a redemptive process. And what I noticed in my self-centered way was that it would help if I learned to check my ego at the door. Berta had to ask again before I reported how Madge was dealing with her current loss.

***

On Tuesday, I arrived just a few minutes before other singers would be coming. Nilda and Madge were sitting together in Madge's favorite corner. We exchanged greetings, but neither seemed anxious to visit. Madge seemed resigned to face Bertram's death away from the family gathering, and look forward to Ralph's visit.

Nilda said, "I'm praying about what you said yesterday." And that was all.

Rachel came in and I went to help move the piano.

***

On Sunday I noted again that it had been several weeks since Madge had been out to church. I knew why, I suppose. How could I expect anything different? Magda was with her mother in the fifth pew. I had been told that she and her husband belonged to the Lutheran Church. Following the service Nilda made sure that Magda and I knew each other, and then said, "I know what you meant. Now I know why and I'm praying for... No, wait a minute, I'm praying into, I'm looking for that forgiveness. Papa and Walter just couldn't be what I wanted them to be. I guess I thought if I did right I could make them what I thought they were supposed to be. Forgiveness takes a lot of letting go, don't it."

I felt the ego boost, that the right part of my advice was heard. And realized immediately that I had my own need of forgiveness prayers, of letting go.

***

Singing time took the Tuesday before Thanksgiving off. So it was only after the call came that I would see Madge again. The call arrived just as we were clearing the table after the Thanksgiving Day turkey dinner. Berta's parents were visiting and we were all going to let the girls show us around their favorite playground at the park. From Nilda's window I had watched other children play there nearly as often as I had been with my daughters there.

The call let us know that while the others played at the swings and slide, I would be across the street at Harstad Hospital, next door to Prairie Manor.

Peter was coming out of the room as I arrived. He seemed to know who I was, and directed me to a family room where we joined Pearl and Peter's wife. They just shook their heads, saying they were glad they'd all extended their visits, but how sad. They were sorry that Ralph was unable to stay longer. We all thought, but couldn't say, that it might be best if she just died right now. Madge's stroke would leave her unable to speak intelligibly, except for an occasional 'damn' when she tried to express herself and no one understood. She would be nearly bedridden for the remaining few months of her life.

In the weeks that followed the stroke, Nilda sat with Madge for an hour or more every morning. She would bring in a daily newspaper, the Billings Gazette or the Bismarck Tribune, read the headlines with her added comments on the virtues of Democrats and depravities of the Republicans. When I suggested that she might be staying too long, Nilda tried to make her visits shorter. Madge got us to understand without clear speech that she wanted Nilda to stay. Nilda insisted that it was not, as I hinted, out of any old feelings of guilt or shame, but out of gratitude for the way Madge helped her to find forgiveness for herself and her deceased loved ones.

My visits became brief times with one sided conversation that began with my saying, "I remember you telling me…"

Epilogue I

The sun was bright in an absolutely clear, blue sky. The February thaw was upon us. On a table at the front of the church's worship center, draped with a white cloth trimmed in lace, among the flowers, were an urn of Madge's cremated remains, the large picture of the family reunion that had hung on her wall, smaller old pictures of Madge with Mr. Carter, with children and even an ancient wedding picture with Elwin. Everyone in that family reunion picture plus a couple new babies, or so it seemed, filed into the church, filling two-thirds of the pews on the left side of the aisle, and a fourth on the right. I became aware (I don't know how I figured it out) that on the left side were all Bowdler and on the right were Carter.

Ruth, Madge's youngest child, had a son who was a minister with youth at a large church in California. He would lead the memorial. As host pastor, I would assist. I wasn't supposed to say much—read a Psalm and the obituary, lead a prayer and let young Derek do the rest.

I added a few personal comments to my obituary reading. I couldn't let "she loved to sew and made all her daughters' dresses" be said without adding something about what that meant for the mercantile, and the whole community during the Depression. I added things like that.

Then I listened as the young pastor preached. I expected to hear some personal and family experiences to reveal something of the gift that Madge's living had been for us. It didn't happen. I was disappointed, to say the least. I was then expected to lead a closing prayer and make two announcements: the lunch first, and the time for immediate family to depart for the interment of ashes at the homestead. The prayer became something more than a few words to send us out. Madge, who had wondered if she lived to be the oldest because she still needed to bring her two families together, still had a word to share. My prayer became hers, with quotation of not staying in hell, remembrance of her discovery of forgiveness where it didn't even seem needed. It had been a dry-eyed family celebration, but as I said "amen" I looked up and saw Nilda near the back of the church with tears running down her cheeks.

I can't be sure it did any good, but the family seemed to mingle and engage in earnest conversation across the divide during the lunch, and even more so later that afternoon.

Ralph and Peter had arranged with the current landowner to bury the urn at Elwin Bowdler's rudely marked grave. This didn't please the Carter descendants, but they accepted it. The burial trip, taken along the route I had explored in September didn't include the grand or great-grand descendants. Only Madge's sons, daughters and spouses went. I hadn't planned to go, but at the last minute Derek insisted that I ride with him. He wanted to know more about the things Madge had told me, and the discoveries that were behind the words in my prayer.

As we neared the fork, where we would have to negotiate a rough trail, I noticed a familiar looking old pickup truck parked along the main road just beyond the turn-off. An old cowboy was leaning on the fender, drinking from a can (Grain Belt, perhaps?). As we passed he tossed the can in the truck box, and climbed in behind the wheel. I twisted around to watch as we bounced up the narrow side road. He joined our procession, making it five vehicles.

Our stopping place was easy to spot this time. A temporary stile of wooden steps had been built over the fence. I was the most recent visitor to the site. It had been many years for some, and never for Henry and Ruth. The slow walk through the muddy ground to the gravesite became an extended tour of reminiscence and wonder.

How much of the ritual to follow had the family planned ahead? Or was it all spontaneous?

The man I knew as Mumble-into-hat stepped up with his rusty shovel. He handed it to Ralph, who turned out one shovelful of turf. Ralph then handed it to Pearl. In silence each family member took a turn, and the hole was large enough. The urn was placed in the ground. Then Derek delivered a five minute elegy that lifted up memories of the real Madge Bowdler Carter. The burial ritual was repeated in reverse with each spooning a shovelful of dirt back into the grave.

I had one more thing to say to Madge. As I ladled a little dirt over the urn, I said, "Your family's love is proving that this is a place that something of you can be again after all. Be at home in the peace that remains for God's people, Madge."

The hugs after were, to my eyes, genuine and indiscriminate. The gulf between the two parts of Madge's family was being bridged.

I was introduced to Tony, but still didn't understand his last name. Tony Mumble-into-hat was a brother of Ralph's wife. Both of us were surprised to see each other there. As we walked toward the cars and visited, he said, "I just want you to know something. It wasn't Townley's fault, really. I blamed him for stirring things up in the old days. But he didn't kill Mr. Bowdler. I'd heard those stories from Ralph and Buddy and all. And I heard from other folks about the League and all the troubles. I guess I just needed somebody to blame. And there's blame enough to spread far and wide. Elwin and his man Townley was just trying to make it better for the farmers. But it was always a losing cause with just a homestead out in this dry country."

We came to his old Chevy pick-up. He reached through the open window and pulled two cans from a cooler. Without asking if I wanted a beer, he popped both open and handed me one. We drank and talked of homesteaders at the prettiest farm you ever did see.

Epilogue II

The week before school started, among fall sports and cheerleading practices, the kids found time to complete the repaint of the wall. They filled in the design they had created with help from Ms. Fielder and her new art teaching aide Roberta Wilson. The new mural included a steam locomotive, grain field, grain elevators, an early combine, a cowboy on horseback roping a calf and another with a branding iron, an oil drilling rig & pumpjack. And at the right end of the wall was a picture of two farmers beside a Model T Ford, both looking at a newspaper with a banner that read 'Nonpartisan Leader'. Below the picture, words were inscribed, "Dedicated to Madge Bowdler Carter, 1886-1982.

ABOUT THE AUTHOR

Kent Elliott recently retired after serving small churches in Montana and Wyoming as a licensed lay minister in the United Church of Christ and pastor in The United Methodist Church. He was ordained a Deacon (Associate Member) in the Yellowstone Conference of the United Methodist Church in 1995. Kent previously worked in services to developmentally disabled people. *I've Seen Dry* is his first novel.

Kent and Barb make their home on a hillside just a little northwest of Boulder, Montana. Their three adult daughters and families also live in Montana.

Kent's work on a second novel is interrupted as often as possible by visits with grandchildren.

ABOUT THE TYPE

This book is set in Century Schoolbook, a typeface designed by Morris Fuller Benton for textbook publishers in the early twentieth century—the era our characters remember. It quickly gained popularity for its easy-to-read quality. You may have learned to read from a primer set in Century Schoolbook.

www.ingramcontent.com/pod-product-compliance
Lightning Source LLC
Chambersburg PA
CBHW070106260626
47160CB00004B/1350